7-13

P9-DHG-894

THE POWER OF HORSES
and Other Stories

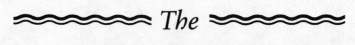

The POWER *of* HORSES

and Other Stories

ELIZABETH COOK-LYNN

Arcade Publishing • *New York*

LITTLE, BROWN AND COMPANY

Copyright © 1990 by Elizabeth Cook-Lynn

All rights reserved. No part of this book may be reproduced
in any form or by any electronic or mechanical means,
including information storage and retrieval systems,
without permission in writing from the publisher, except
by a reviewer who may quote brief passages in a review.

FIRST EDITION

The characters and events in this book are fictitious.
Any similarity to real persons, living or dead,
is coincidental and not intended by the author.

Library of Congress Cataloging-in-Publication Data

Cook-Lynn, Elizabeth.
    The power of horses and other stories / Elizabeth Cook-Lynn. —
1st ed.
        p.   cm.
    ISBN 1-55970-050-5
    1. Sioux Indians — Fiction. I.   Title.
PS3553.05548P6   1990
813'.54 — dc20   89-29862
                                                           CIP

Published in the United States by Arcade Publishing, Inc., New York,
a Little, Brown company

10 9 8 7 6 5 4 3 2 1

FG
Published simultaneously in Canada by
Little, Brown & Company (Canada) Limited

PRINTED IN THE UNITED STATES OF AMERICA

in memory
of Eliza Renville

Contents

Author's Acknowledgments

Grateful acknowledgment is made to the following journals and anthologies, which first printed these stories: *Prairie Schooner, Blue Cloud Quarterly, The Wicazo sa Review, Pembroke Magazine, South Dakota Review, Sinister Wisdom, Earth Power Coming, The Remembered Earth, Seek the House of Relatives,* and *Then Badger Said This.*

THE POWER OF HORSES
and Other Stories

Prologue

When you look East
from Big Pipe's place
you see Fort George; you look
south and see Iron Nation
and you sense a kind of
hollowness
in the endless distance
of the river span
at odds
somehow
with the immediacy
of the steel REA
towers
stalking up and down
prairie hills
yet
as your fingertips
touch the slick leaves
of the milkweed
and roll the juicy leaves
together
it is easy to believe
that this vast region

continues to share its destiny
with a people
who have survived hard winters
invasions
migrations
and transformations
unthought of
and unpredicted

and even easier to know
that the mythology
and history of all times
remains remote
and
believable

Maȟpiyato

One late summer day the old woman and her grandchild walked quietly along the road toward the river, as they had done all their lives. The *(k)unchi* had a large soft blanket tied around her waist and shoulders, and the child swung two small pails, and so, those who might have noticed them knew that they were going to pick wild fruit. The blanket would be thrown beneath buffalo berry bushes to catch the small red fruit as the child, climbing high, would shake the branches vigorously. The small pails would hold the larger tart, wild plums.

The *(k)unchi* wore a black silk kerchief over her white hair, and as she walked, she pulled it closer over her forehead to shade her eyes from the intermittent sun. She shaded her eyes, also, with a slender hand as she looked up into the sky, and the child, attentive to every movement, followed her glance.

The great expanse of the river was shining before them, but, because of a cloud moving across the watery landscape, part of the river looked blue and the other part of it appeared to be dark gray where the shadow of the cloud fell upon it.

"Look at that!" the grandmother said softly in Indian language. And she stood still for a few moments, the child at her side.

"Look, *hunh-he-e-e,*" indicating by the sound of her voice that a sober and interesting phenomenon was taking place right before their very eyes. The child, a steadfast and modest companion of the old woman, knew from long experience about the moments when the stories came on and watched cautiously, leaning to one side so as not to catch the full glare in her eyes.

"That is what we call *mahpiyato,* isn't it?" said the old woman to the child.

"That is what *mahpiyato* really means." She stood as if entranced, her long fingers now touching the fringes of the blanket.

"To say just 'blue' or 'sky' or 'cloud' in English, you see, doesn't mean much. But *mahpiyato* is that Dakotah word which tells us what we are witnessing right now, at this very moment."

She pointed.

"You see, she is blue. And she is gray. *Mahpiyato* is, you see, one of the Creators. Look! Look! *Look at Mahpiyato!*"

Her voice was low and soft and very convincing.

Loss of the Sky

*By the time the United States had entered World
War I, Sioux Indians had then been living on
reservations for a lifetime, and even though
unimaginable changes had been endured, the soul
of the tribe continued in the imagination to be
inherent in* maka, *the earth.*

At the time when descendants of Goethe had begun their
massive, secret march through Belgium, in those years
before the United States entered World War I, there
lived near Fort Pierre, South Dakota, one Joseph
Shields, a fifty-year-old Sioux Indian who in his own
way knew something of the rise of brutal doctrines,
something of the destruction of ancient civilizations,
something of a change of worlds.

The proud owner of two hundred head of horses, he
was a man who strongly reflected his Dakotah heritage,
despite a rather arduous education at Carlisle, that
school for Indians in the East. Through the years, as he
aged, he continued to smoke in the traditional way, to
take the sweat, to carry on long conversations with
friends, and, when he thought no one was watching, he
took his drum out into the prairie hills as the sun rose

and sang the ancient songs of his people, who were called the "sun worshippers of the Plains."

Though he was somewhat Christianized by the Dominican priests who roamed the prairies, as much nomads as any Indians had ever been, Joseph never quite accepted the totality of that faith, never quite believed in the recent god of the strange blackrobes. So it was that whenever the spirit moved him in the old way, he profoundly and reverently sang to the god he knew more intimately.

Though the tyranny of those years would be evident to the world by the crushing of innocent people all over Europe, the perilousness of them seemed remote to old Shields, not at all like the years he remembered from the shadows of his past, when his family hid out in caves along the Missouri River, surreptitiously kept watch on the movements of the U.S. Army troops, wondered aloud about the business of the Seventh Cavalry, Sibley, Thompson, Sheridan, about the new troops they could not identify, who they were and what they wanted here in Sioux Country.

These were not painful years for the old man, not like those of the past nor those to come later. In fact, Joseph had come to the time in his life when he thought of white men and their endless cruelties less and less. Instead, he placed a modicum of good faith in his own immediate world and, more specifically, in the five sons and one daughter his good wife, Ruth, had borne him.

He would go out to the corrals where his sons were working the horses, and with great pride he would watch his middle son, Teo, the finest rider anywhere around, teach his mount to neckrein or bulldog or, as in the case of some of the fresh two-year-olds, to take the saddle.

These were good years, and Joseph thought little about the marauding German armies and the war clouds hanging over the capitals of Europe. The problems of such governments did not concern him. Joseph had never exercised a vote in them, and when the Indian Commissioner came to the reservation from Washington, D.C., to talk of the grandeur of conferring citizenship upon members of the tribe, Joseph listened politely, his eyes directed at the floor. He stared for a long time and never raised his eyes, and then he turned away, walked quietly outside to his team of horses, spoke to them with sureness and authority, and drove them the fifty miles to his place. He never mentioned the matter to his wife, nor to his sons, and if he thought about it at all, it did not take on any grand significance as a noble idea.

So it was that the good weather days passed for Joseph and his family, the days when the breeds and the fullbloods gathered at the fairs to race their horses and socialize at the powwows which followed the competitions, traveling and camping at Fort Pierre, at Rapid City, on through Montana and sometimes as far as Canada, until it was September and time for the sons and daughters to return to the Indian boarding school two hundred miles away.

Every fall, as if the Bureau of Indian Affairs was an

inexorable part of the natural cycle of life, it sent big, open army trucks down to the reservation and swept up every luckless Indian kid along the Crow Creek whose parents hadn't hidden him in the timber.

And then Joseph would be left with the memories of the summer, the echoes of young voices, "*Até . . . ahitonwan*, look here." The horses would get fat and shaggy and wild from little handling through the winter. And Joseph would walk through the silent corrals.

Life went on even then, though, and Ruth would cook the fine soup made of dried corn and *ti(n)psina*, until that awful night when Teo, the middle son, the finest rider anywhere around, walked away from the darkened dormitory for the last time and slipped into the C & NW, whose lonesome whistle had often beckoned him over the years when he would lie in bed on the second floor, unable to sleep, wishing for home.

Teo didn't go home. The school authorities would only come after him as they had done before. Instead, he rode the rails to Chicago, enlisted in the Army, and after a decent training period, was among the 14,000 troops which landed on the shores of France. It was the summer of 1917, seven years before his people were to become U.S. citizens.

Joseph weakened as the years passed. His middle son, the finest rider anywhere around, Teo, had not made it back from France. Joseph kept the paper which told of his son's bravery and his death and that his body would not be coming back. It was the last part of that message which made Joseph an old man.

Inevitably, the proper songs were sung in honor of the young warrior, and for years the anguish of Ruth's wailing songs never left Joseph's memory. Ruth cut her hair and slashed her legs, and after that she never wore the pretty beaded shawls and bright moccasins and hair pieces she loved to make.

Joseph's two hundred head of horses were neglected, became scattered and lost; some of them were stolen, but it did not matter. The old man seemed somehow compelled to sit and gaze into the distance, as if he might see Teo, tall and straight in the saddle, the middle son, the finest rider anywhere around, come over the rise, his arm lifted gently in greeting.

Joseph seldom went into the hills to pray and sing anymore, but when he did, he never failed to weep that the bones of his son, the middle son, the finest rider anywhere around, could not mingle with the bones of his grandfathers.

A Visit from Reverend Tileston

Fifty miles from the nearest town of any size, deep in the bend of the Missouri River, where the *Dakotapi* had made history for generations, lived the Family: Father, a firstborn son whose eyes bore the immutable and unspoken agony of his generation, handsome and strong, a cattleman not so much from choice as from necessity; Mother, a fine quill artist, small-boned and stout, a woman with one crooked elbow caused by a childhood accident, a good cook, accomplished at the piano, guitar, and harmonica, talents she had learned at the government boarding school; Uncle, the Mother's younger brother, a truck driver sometimes, a drunk increasingly often, whenever those inexplicable waves of grief washed over him; Grandmother, Grandfather, and five children ranging in age from three to fifteen years. Uncle's son often lived with the Family, as did the Grandmother's half sister and her husband and their two granddaughters. The Family was part of a small community which had reassembled itself at this place after the violent diaspora and displacement which was endured by this ancient tribe for several generations, the Family all the more closely knit because of this tragedy of recent history as well as the more practical problem of long distances to the few sparse surrounding towns settled a hundred years before by whites anxious to possess land and become rich. The year was 1935, and this was a place where strangers, though alien and undesirable, even called *to'ka*, were largely unthreatening and often ignored, and where strange events were witnessed with inexplicable but characteristic tolerance.

From the graveled road which followed the course of the river, the small, three-room frame house in which the Family now lived, built by the U.S. government for Bureau of Indian Affairs employees in early reservation days and abandoned in later times, looked strangely remote and ageless. It seemed to stare listlessly toward the river's loop, and in winter its long-windowed eyes would be the first to catch a glimpse of the landing of the Canada geese on the cold shores of the whitened, timeless river. It turned its back on the ludicrously inexpedient pyramid-shaped, steel-roofed icehouse, which had once afforded Bureau employees from the East the luxury of iced drinks in the summer as they came to this blistering Dakotah prairie to work "in the Indian service." The icehouse was abandoned now, also, too big and deep to be of any use to the Family except for the summer drying of the pounded meat and berry patties, *wasna,* which would be laid out upon its roof in the sun. During this drying process the children would be set to fanning the flies away with long willows, a task which held their attention a surprisingly brief time. Bored, they would run off in pursuit of more imaginative pastimes, only to be called back as soon as Grandmother discovered their absence.

Also at the rear of the house was a large *tipi,* the color of smoke at the top, streaked with rain, lined with cowhides, comfortable, shaded in late afternoon by the lone pine tree which was, itself, a stranger to the hot Plains country of the Dakotah, itself a survivor of the days when Bureau employees lived there. The children imagined that the tree was brought there by a medicine man and was used in his cures, but it was not a cedar, just a scraggly pine tree which had barely survived hard times. There was a tall hand pump set in the middle of the yard, where Grandmother would kneel to wash the paunch during butchering times, and also a corral set some distance away in the tall pasture grass at the foot of a small rise in the prairie landscape. A huge mound of earth covered a man-made cave, which was complete with wooden steps and a slanting door that had to be picked up and drawn aside. A very large bull snake often found refuge from the blistering sun under one of the wooden steps, stretching himself full-length in the soft, cool, black earth.

Just beyond the cave was a small, white outdoor toilet, another survivor of former times, a product of imag-

inative Public Health Service officials who set about
dotting Indian reservations with these white man's con-
veniences during the early part of the century. Across
the road from the house a gray stuccoed Catholic
church, Saint Anne's, sat with a closed, tight-lipped vis-
age, as though shielding itself from the violent summer
prairie storms which came intermittently, pounding the
gravel and the stucco, flattening the prairie grass. To the
rear of the church lay the remains of the ancestors in a
cemetery which, years later, was said to be occupied by
a den of rattlesnakes.

In summer evenings, the air was often still and quiet,
heavy with moisture. After a late meal, the quiet deepened. The only sound was Grandmother's soft footsteps
as she went back and forth to the kitchen, carrying
dishes from the table. Her ankle-length black dress hid
her bowed legs, and her head was covered, always, with
a black scarf, her long white braids lying on her breast.
Every now and then she stopped to wipe her smooth
face with a white cloth, breathlessly.

"Grandmother, we should cook outside tomorrow,"
said the Youngest Daughter, disheveled and hot, bearing
a load too heavy for her to the kitchen.

The Mother simply sat, one arm outstretched on the
table, the crooked one fanning her face and hair with a
handkerchief. For her it had been a long day, as she and
her sister had spent the afternoon picking wild plums
and buffalo berries along the river.

As the evening came on, the children could be heard
outside, running and chasing one another around the

house and yard, trying to touch each other on the back, stretching away, laughing, now and again falling and crashing into the bushes near the pump. The dogs barked loudly. It was a game the boys never seemed to tire of, even as the sun started to glow in the west and Uncle went outside to begin his nightly summer ritual of starting a smoke-fire, a smudge, to keep the mosquitoes away for the evening.

"*Hoksila kin tuktel un he?*" muttered Uncle as he looked around for one of his nephews to help him gather firewood. "He's never around when you need him."

"Go get some of that wood over there by the back porch." He directed his voice toward the hapless Youngest Daughter, who wrinkled up her nose but went, dutifully, to get the wood. Uncle bent down on one knee to place the sticks and dead leaves just right to produce a heavy smoke. He carefully touched a match to the soft underbrush, and as the smoke rose, he watched, one thumb hooked in his belt. In a few moments smoke filled the air, and members of the Family began to gather for the evening.

They might even see man-being-carried in the sky, thought Uncle, and then he could tell a story if the children felt like listening and could stay awake long enough for the stars to show themselves clearly.

When he straightened up, he was surprised to see a small black sedan some distance down the road, making its way slowly toward them. He kept his eyes on the road to see if he could recognize in the dusk who it was.

He stepped up on the porch and lit a cigarette, the match illuminating the fine, delicate bones of his deeply pocked, scarred face.

Holding the match close for a moment, Uncle said, to no one in particular, "A car's coming."

Cars were rarely seen here on this country road this late in the evening.

As Uncle stood watching, he heard church music, faint at first, and later blaring, and he realized after a few long moments that it was coming from the loud-speaker positioned on top of the sedan.

"On-ward Christian so-o-o-l-diers," sang the re-corded voices of an entire church choir into the quiet evening light as the car came slowly into the river's bend, "with the cross of J-e-e-sus going on before."

Uncle stood with the cigarette in his mouth, his hands in his pockets, as his brother-in-law came out of the house and sat down on the porch step with a cup of coffee. They watched the car approach and listened to the music, now blaring loud enough to get the atten-tion of the children, who stopped running and stood gazing at the strange-looking vehicle.

They stood, transfixed, as the car approached slowly and came to a stop. The loudspeaker fell silent as the driver of the sedan parked the car on the side of the road near the mailbox and, with great cheer, stepped from the car, waving and smiling. He was a man of about forty with a broad, freckled face. He was per-spiring heavily, and he made his way down the short path from the road to the house. Behind him came two women dressed in blue-and-white flowered dresses, brown stockings, and flat brown shoes; their faces, like pale round melons, were fixed with broad smiles. They all carried black leather-bound Bibles, the kind with red-tipped pages.

"Boy, it's hot!" said the fortyish, freckled man as he held out his hand in greeting. The Father did not look at him, nor did he get up. He put the cup to his lips and sipped coffee quietly, ignoring the intrusion with sullen indifference. Uncle kept his hands in his pockets, and with his tongue he shifted his cigarette to the other side of his mouth.

Ignoring what was clearly a personal affront by the two men on the steps, the freckled man said, "Say, that's a good trash-burning operation there," turning to the children standing beside the smudge. The children looked first at the smudge and then back at the perspiring man, and, silently, they shook hands with him. Grasping the unwilling hand of the Youngest Daughter, standing a few feet away, the man, in a loud voice asked, "Is your mommy home, honey?" Nearly overcome with embarrassment, she said, "Yeh, she's in there," and gestured toward the door.

"Well," the man said as he turned and walked up the steps slowly, avoiding the Father and the Uncle still mutely positioned there, "we've come a long way with the message of hope and love we've got right here," and he patted the black leather-bound book he carried. As he tapped on the screen door, the Mother appeared, and the freckled man quickly opened the door, stepped inside, and held it open for the two smiling women who accompanied him to squeeze inside and in front of him.

"I'm Sister Bernice," began the plumper of the two women, "and this is Sister Kate . . . ?" Her voice trailed off as if she had asked a question. When there was no response, she turned to the freckled man, and putting her hand on his elbow, she said, "And we're here with Reverend Tileston."

Taking a deep breath, the Reverend said to the Mother in his kindliest voice, "Ma-a'aam, we'd like to pray with you," and there in the middle of the room, he knelt and began paging through his Bible, motioning for the women to join him as he knelt. His two companions quickly dropped to their knees, and the plump one said to the Mother, "Please pray with us, sister," and the Mother, after a brief, uncertain moment, also knelt. Espying the Grandmother and her half sister peering at them curiously from the kitchen doorway, the Reverend quickly got up and led them to the middle of the room, saying, "Come on with us, Granny, pray with us," and the two old women, too, with great effort, got to their knees. The Youngest Daughter, having followed the astonishing trio into the house, stood beside her grandmother and looked expectantly at the perspiring freckled man as he fell to reading from the leather-bound book:

"With ALL our energy we ought to lead back
ALL men to our most MER-ci-ful Re-DEE-mer,"

he read. His voice rose:

"He is the Divine Cons-o-o-oler of the afflicted";

Youngest Daughter hung her head, copying the attitude of the visitors.

"To rulers and subjects alike He teaches lessons of true holiness,"

the Reverend sucked in air:

"unimpeachable justice, and,"

he breathed again:

"generous charity."

The Reverend's voice seemed to fill the cramped little room, and Sisters Bernice and Kate, eyes tightly closed, murmured, "Amen," louder and louder with each breath the minister took.

Youngest Daughter glanced first at her Mother, then her Grandmothers, who were kneeling shoulder to shoulder, faces impassive, eyes cast to the floor. Then, the Reverend closed the book, raised his arms, and recited from memory, Proverbs:

"Hear O children, a father's instruction," he shouted. "Be attentive, that you may gain understanding! Yea, excellent advice I give you; my teaching do not forsake."

One of the dogs, hunching itself close to the screen door, began to whine.

The Reverend continued to shout: "When I was my father's child, frail, yet the darling of my mother, he taught me, and said to me: 'Let your heart hold fast my words! Keep my commands, do not forget; go not astray from the words of my mouth.' "

His arms fell and his voice softened as he uttered the last phrase, opened his eyes, and looked, unseeing, at the little girl, his gaze moist and glittering. The dog's whine became more persistent, his tone now pitched higher to match the Reverend's, and he began to push his nose against the screen door, causing it to squeak loudly.

The Reverend Tileston looked into the passive faces of the Mother and the Grandmothers, and as he said, "The beginning of wisdom is: get wisdom; at the cost of ALL-L-L-L you have," his arm swung dangerously close to the unfortunate dog, who flattened his ears and pushed himself closer to the door.

"Get understanding," Reverend Tileston urged. "Forsake her not and she will preserve you; love her, and she will safeguard you; extol her, and she will exalt you; she will bring you honors if you embrace her; she will put on your head a graceful diadem; a glorious crown will she bestow upon you."

The words seemed to roll from his tongue, and Youngest Daughter imagined shining crowns placed upon the heads of her Mother and her Grandmothers, still kneeling stiffly and impassively. She was thrilled with the sound of the English words, though she knew she didn't comprehend their meaning. It was like the times when Felix Middle Tent, the well-known Dakotah orator, made his speeches at the tribal council meetings she sometimes attended with her father, when he used his most eloquent and esoteric Dakotah vocabulary, oftentimes derisively referred to by Uncle as "jaw-breakers."

As the Reverend's hefty arm again swept the room, the whining dog lurched backward and fell against a large pail of buffalo berries which Mother had left on the porch that late afternoon. Terrified, the dog leapt into the second pail of plums, scattering them wildly, then he dashed under the porch, where he set up a mournful howl. The boys, who had been listening at the side window, fled into the bushes, laughing and screaming.

The Mother and Grandmothers, surprised and shocked at this turn of events but bent upon retrieving the day's pickings, swept past the astonished, speechless minister, shouting abuse at the now thoroughly miserable dog, and the screen door slammed behind them. Youngest Daughter was left looking into the disappointed faces of the Reverend and his companions. She smiled.

Forced by these circumstances to admit that the spiritual moment was lost, the Reverend Tileston got to his feet and ushered Sisters Bernice and Kate out of the house, carefully picking a path through the berries covering the porch. He was relieved that the Father and Uncle were nowhere to be seen, and he turned at the last step and made a final effort, saying, "Meditate, Mothers, on the Scriptures, have knowledge of them, for they are the food which sustains men during times of strife."

The women, engrossed in saving the berries, didn't hear him.

His final proselytizing gesture, the attempted distribution of printed pamphlets, was also ignored.

Their composure now completely shattered, the trio which bore God's Word into this obscure bend in the river found its way, falteringly, to the sedan, switched on the loudspeaker, and drove slowly away.

Youngest Daughter looked after them as they ventured deeper into the curve along the river, and the faint echo of "with the cross of Jee-e-sus . . ." rang in her ears. After a moment she went to find Uncle, who would tell her a story about the star people and how the four blanket carriers once helped him find his way home from a long and difficult journey.

She hoped that the Reverend knew about the blanket carriers.

A Family Matter

A vague restlessness woke Anita, and on impulse she got up and opened the bedroom window. It was just before dawn, when the light of the moon had faded and shadows fell darkly upon the steep hills and pines and the river lay silent and still.

Today she was going to Fort Hall.

Crouching on her knees, Anita peered into the darkness and felt the presence of the geese just before she heard them. Hurrying, stroking the air powerfully, purposefully, the huge flock hung for a moment above her window, and then, individually, they began their lonely, awkward cries to each other, calling their names and telling stories and moving ponderously into the heavy fog which lay in the distance across the hills. Unaccountably, hot tears stung Anita's eyes and her nose. Her cheeks ached. Quickly, she got up and switched on a light in the hall and went to the kitchen to make coffee.

She poured the hot coffee into a thermos, went back to the bedroom, and dressed in the semidarkness. She went over to her husband, motionless in the pretense of sleep, his arms raised to cover his eyes. "I'm going," she said. She sat still on the side of the bed for a few moments, until she realized that he wasn't going to say anything to her, and then she put on her coat, took the thermos from the kitchen table, and left the house. She drove her car carefully away in the drizzling rain, and she knew that Ray was lying there listening to her leave.

An hour later she stopped just outside of St. Maries and parked her red Nova at a rest stop alongside the freeway. It's the first of November, she thought, and she felt chilled as she walked to the roadway bathhouse, the sky and the land shrouded in gray light. She searched the sky for the sun, weak and pale beneath the moist clouds, and decided silently, This day's not going to get any better than this.

The toilet was empty except for a short, white-haired woman, who smiled and adjusted her belt as Anita walked to the narrow booth.

"Too much coffee, I guess," said the white-haired lady pleasantly, and they both nodded.

Moments later, as they left the bleak, quiet bathhouse, the woman, smiling brightly, said *do you mind if I ask you a question sure said Anita You're Indian aren't you yes well said the woman I've known a lot of good Indians and there's nothin' to be ashamed of we're from Phoenix as if that explained something and we run a grocery and tourist stop and we've had a lot of good Indian boys work for us and you don't need to be ashamed of that.*

In order not to be rude, Anita strolled with the woman to the curb and feigned a politeness she did not feel.

"Where you headed?" asked White Hair.

"Fort Hall."

"Oh, do you live there?"

"No, I used to be married there. I'm just going there to get my two sons and bring them back with me."

"Oh, how nice! Well . . . ," said White Hair, who noticed that her husband had started the car engine, "have a nice trip," and she smiled and waved.

Anita felt small and remote as she pulled out onto the freeway. The whistling wind rising about the faulty car window reminded her of the sound of huge goose wings flapping. White Hair's "how nice" hissed in her ears, and she tried to organize her vision about herself as the mother of her two sons and the wife of Ray and the ex-wife of Victor and the daughter-in-law of Rosina and the stepdaughter of John Thunder and . . . and . . . she tried to organize these thoughts about herself around White Hair's words, though she knew them to be superficial and secular. How nice that I'm going to get my sons after a year's rehab at the treatment center and two years working as a nurse's aide and two years married to Ray. How nic-c-c-e! For five years my sons

haven't laid eyes on me, and now I'm going to get them.
Yes-s-s. How nic-c-c-e!

"Rain is expected to continue," the radio announcer
proclaimed. "Highs will be around fifty to fifty-four degrees throughout the day and lows are expected to reach
twenty-eight degrees. And now, here's George Jones, the
best of the country singers, and he's fallen on hard
times. Here's 'He Stopped Loving Her Today.' "

Anita thought vaguely about her own decline and
weary deterioration and considered that it had been inevitable, perhaps, like the fading of the dim November
sun she now glimpsed over her left shoulder as she
drove, the yellow outlines of the great *tunkashina* fading
into impotence as the distance from the earth widened,
more feeble and indistinct than at any other time of the
year.

As the rain glittered and country music filled the air,
the red Nova slipped through the hills of northern
Idaho, and the hours passed and the woman driving did
not stop but once for gas until the headlights fell upon
one of the three grocery stores at Fort Hall, Idaho. She
bought some cheese, crackers, and milk and went
straight to the motel to eat a quick snack and fall into
a heavy, soundless sleep.

Toward morning she dreamed of two small boys
walking along looking for a bear. While they were walking, they heard something coming after them. When
they looked around, they saw that it was their mother's
head. "Where are you going?" asked the head. The chil-

dren became afraid and ran away and climbed into a tree. Their mother's head followed them and began shaking the tree, and just when the tree was about to fall, a voice from the treetop said to the children, "Sit, quickly, in the bird's nest," and as they climbed into the bird's nest, the wind bore it off swiftly. The head wept loudly.

Anita woke with a start as the weeping sounds of her dream changed to the murmur of the autumn wind moaning in her ears, and she lay in the narrow bed, exhausted and spent. She thought about Ray and wished that he would have consented to come with her.

Leaves swept in bunches by the wind covered the sidewalk as she entered the tribal building and asked the secretary to confirm her appointment with Emil White Horn and the tribal family counselors.

When she walked into the court chambers, she noticed that her children were not present, only their grandmother, Rosina, and she felt sharply disappointed for a moment. Then she felt her hands go cold as she realized that something was wrong.

She looked up, scanning the judge's chambers quickly, and she saw Emil striding toward her, and as he held out his hand to her, he said, "Anita, something's happened here. You see, the boys didn't want to come and they don't want to see you and so we've got them in Smokey's office down the hall. We thought we'd just go ahead and hear some testimony and maybe . . . you know . . . these family matters . . ."

"No," cried Anita, and she jerked her hand away from him.

"They're *my kids* and nobody's going to turn them against me now and it's already been decided that they would come with me . . ."

"Look, Anita," pleaded Emil. "Jesus, it's been . . . how long? Five? . . . six years? . . . Jesus, Anita, give those kids a chance. They don't even know you."

"That's not it, Emil, that's not it." Panic rose in her. "You know that's not it. That old woman, there . . ." and she pointed to the children's grandmother, Victor's mother, Rosina. "She's the one! She's turned them against me. She never did like me and she has made them afraid of me. That's what happened."

By this time, Anita was moving down the hall toward the office where her two children were being held. Rosina, silent and fearful, moved along with her, the two women now facing each other, Emil being drawn behind them as though sleepwalking. Finally, Emil found his voice and said, "Anita, come into the judge's chambers here, and we can talk about this . . ."

Now Anita had reached Smokey's office, and, turning her attention inward, she softly opened the door and saw her two sons, now almost grown, Jay Richard — he was three when she last held him in her arms — and Victor, Jr. — she had always called him Chunskay — had been four when she had last seen him. Looking at them as though from a great distance, she knew what fine men they would become, and tears welled in her throat. She drew in her breath, and with great restraint, she said their names softly. As she stood before them, she could see the fear and anxiety in their eyes, and she said, "Don't be afraid," and then, "You know me, don't you?"

Young Victor pulled Jay Richard to him as his mother reached out toward them, and they both pressed themselves against the corner of the desk.

"Oh, my God," said Anita. "Look what she's done. Look what she's done to them."

And she moved her hands toward her forehead and wiped the perspiration away. She stroked her hair at her temples in a gesture of anguish. Still looking at her sons, she began speaking in the tribal language of her ancestors: *"Taku eniciapi he? ni Dakotapi?* Yes . . . you are my sons and you are Dakotahs and your relatives are significant people. You must remember who you are."

It was a plea, but Jay Richard and Victor, Jr., looked back at her uncomprehendingly. Slowly they moved toward their grandmother and each took a position beside her and, finally, Chunskay said to the mother he had forgotten, "We don't want to go with you. Don't make us go with you."

The misery in the young mother's eyes was too much for Emil, himself almost moved to tears, and he took her arm and led her into the hallway.

His voice choked with emotion, he said, "Look, Anita . . . we can work this out. We'll have to . . ."

But, before he could finish, Anita lifted her head and pushed his arm away and said, "No . . . no . . . ," and she walked away from him. She didn't look back at him as she left the building, though if she had she would have seen that his eyes were filled with sorrow.

As she drove north, she noticed that the snow had started. Soft, large flakes streaked and slanted through the air like a funnel with its tip just in front of her eyes. A long angle of geese zigzagged through the gray sky toward her, and just before it fell away, she thought it seemed close enough to touch.

La Deaux

"*Wichinchila waste wa luha,*" he said to her father, lifting his chin at the little girl. "You have a good girl there." He said this every time they came, yet the father smiled and was pleased.

They didn't know this man well, but then, nobody did. His name was Jack La Deaux, and his face looked like "twenty miles of bad road," her brother used to say. He spoke French as well as he spoke the dialect of the Tetonais, maybe better, and also some English. Her father used to go to La Deaux's place along the river because he had good sweet corn in July, and they could take a wagonload of it home for the women to dry and parch for winter store.

La Deaux was a distant man, as unknowable as the land and the past, and few of the Indians around socialized with him. He wore the leather beaded moccasins and leggings old Sioux women made, but there was no other evidence that he had a woman. Otherwise, he seemed to live alone with two bird dogs who yelped and moaned and cried whenever someone came into the yard.

He was a strange figure, walking everywhere he went, apparently not coveting the horses in which Sioux men took pride, and he was never without a hunting rifle at his side. It had the longest barrel the little girl had ever seen.

Her father would sit on the ground and smoke with La Deaux while she and her brother took their time loading the wagon full of corn. He would tell her father rumors of the bone keeper's feast out near the Black Hills, and when the corn was nearly loaded, they would all share the strong coffee he always made.

If they didn't see La Deaux for many weeks, it seemed as natural as when they saw him frequently. But one October morning, she awoke early and heard her father talking quietly to her grandmother about something which had frightened him during the night. She followed him outdoors and watched as he looked up at the feather-plumed clouds in the sky, and the motion of them seemed somehow ominous. Without understanding, she knew that something terrible had happened. Under her breath she spoke La Deaux's name and her father said, "*Cheyá šni yo,*" but she hid her face and cried anyway, ashamed that she couldn't help herself.

There was no sound except that of the wagon wheels as they rolled over the hard earth into the barren yard, the dogs strangely silent, crouching in the dark places under the porch, the flies unseasonably thick around the door. She stayed in the wagon, fearful of death, and watched her father go inside the cabin. He was still there when men from the Agency came and stood outside the door, and they all waited for her father's song to end. When they brought La Deaux out, her father was carrying the old breed's long-barreled rifle and, oddly, his tobacco pouch. La Deaux was wrapped in many blankets and his face had been painted, "So they will know who he is," her father told her. She never saw the bullet hole, nor did she know until much later that he had been dead and alone for nearly two weeks.

Last Days of a Squaw Man

When I looked out of the motel window, I saw Calvin coming across the parking lot, two six-packs of beer under each arm, the index finger of his right hand curled around the handle of a huge green bottle of T. J. Swann, and a couple of sacks of booze stuffed inside his shirt. He was talking and laughing, but just then I couldn't hear what he was saying. Behind him, two of our sisters, Pearl and Theresa, were half-carrying another brother, Tony, so drunk his head bounced back and forth and his black raincoat, as black as his long shiny hair, flapped around his thin body. Tony's arms were around the shoulders of the girls, and all together they lurched toward a first-floor room. Wendell, his hands stuffed in his jeans, tagged along behind, a middle brother even now as an adult, still the follower.

From where I was standing on the second-floor landing of the Motel 6, I heard Calvin say as they drew closer, "Oh, shit. I'm gonna drop this! God damn it, I'm gonna drop it!" Somehow, he hung on, hunching his head down into his shoulders and taking mincing steps, gripping his precious cargo as if his life depended on it. He struggled in this fashion toward the door and leaned against it, slowly sliding everything downward toward the dusty floor mat.

"Tone-e-e-e," I heard Pearl shriek and saw her pushing him upward, trying to make him stand on his own. "Hey, Tone," she pleaded.

"Where's the fuckin' key, Calvin? Have you got the goddamned key?"

"Hell no. I ain't got no key!"

"Where the hell's Emily?"

"Hey!" Calvin hollered and started pounding on the door. "Hey, Emmie."

Just then my sister-in-law, nervous as a cat, opened the door, and she helped her husband haul his treasures inside. The girls lifted Tony in, and the door closed.

Muffled, shrill swearing; laughter, raucous behind the door.

I turned back into our room toward my husband, tall and rawboned, half-dressed, standing in front of the mirror pulling the floss between his teeth and looking upward into his mouth.

"Good God! You should see them!" I slammed the door. I flung myself on the bed and started to cry and talk at the same time. Alex turned around, still flossing, and looked at me.

"They're just drunk!" I said. "All of them! God, you should see them. Staggering. Cussing!"

I got up from the bed and threw the door open as if I were going to holler into the night. Instead, I said in a pitiful voice, "I'm so mad! I'm so-o-o mad, Al. And ashamed! Grown men and women, forty years old, with children of their own who are grown men and women. Staggering around like a bunch of worthless . . ."

Turning, I grabbed a cigarette from my case, lit it, and dragged on it like a dying man sucking for air. The rush opened my lungs, and I felt better almost instantly.

I felt sorry for myself and the whole grousing lot of us. I felt sorry for our mother, long cold in her grave, dead at forty-two. Her disappointment. Her grief and depression.

We were just kids when we clustered around her death bed at the reservation Public Health Hospital, all ten of us, and heard her say, "*Cheyá šni!*" "Don't cry! I've lived long enough!" We really didn't know what it meant at the time, but later, after I'd married, had children and grandchildren, I recognized her final admonition for what it was: the exhausted utterance of a woman who had lived an unbearable, futile life with a man so warped she knew that his children would never be able to escape him, and when she looked out toward the interminable years stretching before her, she simply gave it up, gladly and without regret. In doing so, she left us on our own and I wondered how much I resented her for that.

I pulled on the cigarette and stepped softly over to

the motel railing just outside the door. I looked out at the lights of this small, prairie city, a town inhabited by busted cowboys, long-haul truckers, their vain women and wasteful children; lone Indians, failed and heartsore, fed up with the duplicity that overtook their lives when they came here but too broken to find a way back home to live with their relatives, fundamentalist preachers who had the sure answers to all the wrong questions. I recognized my past here, standing in the cool night air, the yellow light of the motel flowing all around the doorway. And the tears dried stiffly on my cheeks. I couldn't smile and wondered if I'd ever smile again.

I turned back into the room and lay down on the bed, listening to the voices and the noises from the other rooms in the tiny motel complex. At midnight, long after Alex had slipped into a steady, warm, snoring sleep, I watched the changing purple, reddish lines behind my eyelids, felt the closeness of the still, dark drapes which kept out the light from the streetlamp, and contemplated the faint sounds of night. My thoughts turned to the past, and I imagined the darkness of the treeless prairie which surrounded the two-room house where we grew up near Bad Canyon, when our mother was still alive, and I heard the wind filling up the vast spaces all around us.

I wanted to reach toward Alex and ask him to help, but he was turned away, stiff and immovable. Instead, Russell kept coming toward me, his lower lip bulging with

*a wad of tobacco, his cold blue eyes like sunken marbles
under his massive shock of gray hair.*

*"You whore," he shouted into my innocent nine-
year-old face. Putting thin arms up in front of my face,
I pleaded, "Daddy, don't. Daddy. Please." But the
stinging leather of the quirt caught me on the chin, and
it came down again and again on my back and legs. I
sank to the ground and whimpered.*

*"Don't you pull that pitiful stuff on me, you little
slut. Devil! You little piece of shit!"*

*He turned his head and spit a long, stringy stream
of brownish saliva and phlegm. It drooled on his thin
blue lips and he licked it off, showing his yellow, rotted
teeth, and what was left of it hung on his straggly beard.*

Russell most often came like that. Sometimes he
would come smiling, softly pointing fingers, stroking,
caressing, saying, "I'm gonna get you." And, "I'll get
you yet." And I would run. Run and run. Away. As far
as I could get. One time I ended up on Aunt Irene's
porch, barefoot in the snow. Lots of times I crouched
half the night, wild-eyed, breathless, in the horse's stall
in the barn and watched the yellow glow from the flash-
light seek me out.

*"Oh, God. Jesus. Mary. You must help. I won't ever be
bad. I'll pray. I'll pray."*

Half-asleep and half-awake, I became aware that the
cussing and laughing had stopped and the drapes started

swaying. Loud pounding on the door shook the thin walls of the cheap motel.

"Get up! Gracie! Gracie! Get out here. Hurry up!"

Stumbling in the darkness, I reached the window and pulled back the drapes. Pearl was standing there, her hands to her face.

"Please, Grace. Help!"

"Oh, God. Now what," I whispered, aware of Alex moving on the other side of the bed, his bare feet hitting the floor.

"Open up!" *Pound. Pound. Pound.*

Why is it always me? Why always calling me?

I threw the door open and Pearl rushed in, grabbing me by the shoulders. Clinging to me, she said, "I think Tony's dead, Gracie. We can't wake him up. He took something. Some pills, I think. And we can't get him up. He's dead. He's dead. I just know he's dead," she wailed loudly.

Why wasn't I frightened? Why didn't I care? Her arms around me were warm and sweaty.

By the time we got downstairs, I was fully awake. Cal was passed out on the floor, his hat crumpled beneath him, his mouth open and slack. But his snoring told me he was alive.

I stood over Tony, lying on the bed. His dark skin was the color of wet, decaying leaves, and he looked for all the world as if he wasn't breathing. Grabbing his arm, I couldn't get a pulse. I looked at Theresa, sitting drunkenly in a chair by the desk.

"He's cold, Theresa. Get a warm rag! Get it on his face!"

She sat as though in a stupor, eyes half-closed, and didn't move. Couldn't move, perhaps. A recent widow, with three teen-aged children, she was the "prissy" one among us. Sent off by the nuns to the Coast to take up religious studies, she had rebelled at seventeen, married an army recruiter, and lived a white woman's life in one of the suburbs of St. Paul. Looking as drunk as I've ever seen anyone look, yet still sitting upright, she stared at me stupidly.

"Why in the hell don't you call nine-one-one?" I raised my voice toward Pearl, still standing behind me acting as if she was scared out of her wits.

"How dumb can you get?" I reached for the telephone.

Pearl grabbed the receiver from my hands and said, "Don't. He told me when we picked him up at the airport tonight that they were lookin' for him out of Denver. He don't need the cops!"

"Get ahold of him, then," I said, lifting his skinny body into a sitting position. "We're gonna have to walk him."

Alex held the door open, and we struggled with him out into the night air and began walking him around and around in the parking lot, between the cars, up and down the sidewalk. Within a few minutes, he moaned and threw up all over my shoes and the front of my pajamas. Holding his wrist, I took his arm off my shoulders and threw him forward in disgust. Pearl, off-balance, barely caught him but held tight.

"Hey, Gracie!" she whined. "Whaddaya doin'?"

It was then that I recalled my mother's words. "*You are responsible to your relatives. All of your relatives must be taken care of.*" It was meant, I suppose, as some kind of philosophical idea expressed by the wise men of her people, our people, the Dakotapi, a notion about how to survive the world, a tribal law by which to live.

As I raced back to my room, I was struck by the thought that if my mother had really believed in the tribal laws of her people, she would never have married that white man that we'd all come here now to bury, would never have lived the way that she did for half of her life. She would never have sent us off relentlessly, year after awful year, to the Catholic boarding schools (a different one every couple of years) hundreds of miles from her presence and her own relatives. If it were so important that we honor the tribal customs, why, then, should we be educated by priests and nuns who knew nothing of our ways but, more importantly, felt they were superior to us?

The education of Indians and half-Indians, always a matter of some ambiguity, had very little to do with what was wrong with our family, I thought; yet, because we were sent away to mission boarding schools and spent only the summers at home with our parents (and sometimes not even that), we always displayed, I thought, a distorted sense of who we were as relatives to one another. And so, the admonition of my mother's which now rang in my ears, as I rushed off to the bathroom with my youngest brother's vomit streaming down my legs, seemed foolish and feeble. Why did it come to mind at all? Especially now?

Now all together, except for two ailing sisters and one brother, for the first time in ten years, we found ourselves unable to stand one another; indeed, we found ourselves totally intolerant of one another and unfit to spend even a few hours in social and familial agreement.

When I got to my room, I tore off my pajamas and stuffed them into a plastic bag, trying not to gag, determined to dispose of them in the garbage and be rid of them forever. In the shower I turned the water on as hot as I could stand it.

Tears ran down my cheeks, and I held my face toward the hot spray.

The wad of tobacco juice splashed me in the eye as I crawled toward Tony's broken body. Poor Tone. He lay as though there was no life left in him, scratches in the dust around him showing how he had writhed beneath the whip. "Don't, Daddy," I cried. "Don't hit him any more."

He was just little then. Probably no more than four. Tiny arms and legs flailing in the dust. Drenched in sweat, I grabbed little Tony and lay on top of him. SLAP. SLAP. SLAP. I didn't flinch. Gritting his teeth, Russell turned away in disgust. My back stung as if hot oil was being poured on it. Don't cry! "Go ahead," he said. "Protect him all you want. I know I'll get him."

He cleared his throat and spit and lurched toward the house, where my baffled mother lurked behind the curtain. "You goddamned lazy little shits," he muttered, "sooner or later . . ." He turned on the skinny hound dog which had come out from under the wooden porch, sniffing, whining. He struck it with the whip, and the dog yelped, turned, and slunk away.

The hot spray stung my back, and as I lathered my shoulders with soap, I felt again the marks, though they couldn't have still been there. That was years ago, and, surely, they would have disappeared with the passage of time. All pain disappears, they say, in time. Yes.

"Good-bye," I whispered, weeping into the water spray, squeezing my eyes shut. "Good-bye."

I stepped out of the shower, and, dripping wet, grabbed the bottle of green mouthwash from my cosmetic bag. I took a huge mouthful, gargled, and spit it in the basin. I washed my hands and wrists at the sink, rinsing, rinsing, rinsing. Wrapping a towel around me, I lay down on the bed, exhausted, trembling, and seething with anger.

By eleven-thirty in the morning we had all more or less pulled ourselves together to meet with our deceased father's surviving spouse, Bonnie, to make arrangements for the funeral and burial. Calvin, the eldest brother present, was drunk on his feet but managing to pretend that he was purposeful and in charge. He sat across the table from the mortician, spoke quietly about the weather, and agreed to the service, the preacher, the songs of Christian probity to be sung for a man he had hated since the day he was born.

Facing him, Calvin gripped the wrench. Furtively, they circle one another. "You son of a bitch," Calvin rasped, his teeth clenched. "You touch her again and I'll kill ya." Pearlie stood next to the old Dodge, dirty tears streaked across her face and down the white blouse ripped and hanging away from her breast. She was wailing loudly, begging them to stop. Russell stood his distance, the quirt shaking and snaking in his powerful right hand. He began to strike it toward his grown son, digging into the dirt near his feet. Menacing. Lethal. I saw in Calvin's eyes, black as pitch, a mixture of shame and fear and murderous rage.

The funeral home seemed so quiet and civil. Tony, still the color of spoiled avocados, sat shakily next to Pearl, who had put on black stockings, black shoes, and a skin-tight black dress for this occasion of mourning. Out of respect? For whom? Surely not the man whose body was lying in state in the outer rooms here, in death benign, in life so barbarous. Theresa, skinny and tight-lipped, wore a pink suit and white gloves. Wendell wore gray. Subdued and sedate. A facade of gentility covering the deepest sores of rancor and venomousness.

With Bonnie beside him and the rest of us hovering near, Calvin said clearly, "But we won't have him buried next to our mother. She," nodding his head toward

Bonnie, "will have to find someplace else to put him."

Bonnie's face crumpled and her two blonde daughters moved closer to her. One took her hand lovingly and patted it.

"He don't belong there on the reservation," Calvin went on, his face showing neither compassion nor hatred.

"We're here for the funeral service, and we wanted to help out for that, but . . . you know . . . you know . . ." he faltered and stopped. Why stop now? Go ahead, Cal. I'm not surprised, I thought silently. In the end, Russell always cowed Calvin.

The mortician spoke. "I understand." He sounded so reasonable.

Then, "Now, I understand, also, that there is an empty place next to your mother, Russell's first wife, in the family plot on the reservation. And, really, Bonnie has no other place for him."

"Think of that, folks. She really has no other place to put him."

"And," he continued softly, "she has no money."

Sunshine flooded the room, which smelled like fresh, wet roses. The floor was covered with a deep-pile carpet, and the chairs around the room were the finest maple, with cushioned seats of red tweed.

"Yeah," Calvin said finally. "All's I'm saying is that he will not be buried beside our mother."

"Is that what you all want?" asked the mortician, looking around the room at the rest of us. We averted our eyes, looked down at our feet, shrugged.

Why were we here? What are we doing here? I wondered. This man who was our father, our progenitor, the husband of our mother and after that the husband of Bonnie, was a vicious and loathsome brute. A white man, he abused his Indian children and shocked his wife into submission every day of our miserable lives. He was a white man who had married a tribal woman, lived on the lands of her ancestors, and mistreated her, family members, and his own children, until the entire community refused to have anything to do with them. He was called a "squaw man," and the family lived in isolation and fear.

Why are we here, ritualizing his death? Do we think that we can bring meaning to such a life through such final dramatizations? At least one among us did not think so. When I telephoned our sister in Fort Yates earlier in the week, she had said, "I'm not coming, Gracie."

"I could send you a bus ticket or an airline ticket, Tootie. You know, in only a couple of hours . . ."

"Get this straight, Grace. I am not coming in any case. Not under any conditions. NOT — FOR — ANY — REASON. Have you got that?"

"Yes."

And I knew as I hung up the phone that she was the only truthful one of the bunch. It made me wish that I had the guts to refuse to be a part of all this. Her seriousness made me certain that what we were doing as a family coming here to bury him, to say the last words over his miserable remains, was perverse and obscene.

I was beginning to understand that we were not a family and perhaps had never been one. We were, instead, a disease-producing organism, a pathogen if you will, and we had grown stronger throughout the years because we clung to one another out of some misguided pity and compassion for each other, and we clung to the memory of what we might have been. We were the victims and didn't know it, still prisoners of our own deformed love of ourselves. It was not Russell's hatred for us nor ours for him that held us captive. It was our own impossible need to love each other.

I stood behind Calvin, close to tears.

Calvin held his ground.

"He's a white man," I heard him say finally. "We do not want to bury him next to our mother and her relatives."

Bonnie sniffled into an Ivory Soap–scented handkerchief, her freckled hands puffy and red. Calvin got up and left the funeral parlor, and I knew that he was headed for what was left of that fifth of Black Velvet. The rest of us left the building right behind him, got in our cars, and drove back to the motel. The funeral was set for nine in the morning.

All afternoon, I flipped through magazines in the motel room, kept furtive watch on the activities of my siblings in the downstairs rooms, and listened to the muffled sounds of their trauma. Toward evening, I went downstairs, knocked on the door, and joined them.

"Hell, c'mon in!" yelled Calvin. I opened the door

and saw him lying with his shirt off on the floor in front of the television.

I felt that I was tiptoeing as I made my way across the room.

"Bonnie asked if we wanted a rosary said for tonight, you know," I said.

"Shit," muttered Pearl from the bathroom doorway, where she was leaning over the sink, trying, unsuccessfully, to pluck her eyebrows. She had changed from the black dress of mourning to jeans and a light blue T-shirt with Old Fart's Wife emblazoned on the front of it in black letters. Her husband, the "old fart," one presumed, a meat cutter in Sioux City, had not accompanied her on this trip. He was Pearl's third husband, and I had never met him.

"Hey," Calvin shouted to Emily, "go out there and get some more ice. We ain't got enough ice."

I went over to the desk and started mixing myself a drink.

"So," he said, turning to me. "You're not too good for us, huh?"

Starting that again, are you, Calvin, I thought. I took a good look at him and realized he was very drunk. He was standing now and his knees started to buckle, but he straightened them and stood, trembling.

"I don't drink very much any more, Cal," I said, as if in need of some kind of excuse or explanation of myself.

Sensing my apologetic stance, Calvin got more aggressive.

"Why in the hell didn't you say something to that goddamned funeral home guy, Gracie? Didn't want to look bad, or something?"

"Well . . ."

"Jeezuz!"

"I figured you were drunk enough to do it for all of us, I guess," I said sarcastically, quietly taking a sip of my orange juice and vodka.

"Oh yeah? I'm drunk, huh?"

I didn't say anything.

"Tough shit, Grace!"

Emily came back with the ice. Smiling. Glad to be of use. Unaware of the impending quarrel.

Calvin grabbed the plastic pail from her and hurled it across the room with great force. As he did so, his bladder let go and he peed all over himself. For just a moment, he stood as if in shock.

"Calvin!" Emily cried, looking at me with scared, rabbit eyes.

"Hey, Cal," I shouted and reached for him, suddenly solicitous and worried. "You've got a little accident here." I started to help him sit down next to the desk. He was too drunk to know what had happened and he looked down at his crotch uncomprehendingly.

Just then Pearl came out of the bathroom with a silly grin on her face, lurching past the bed and shaking him. She turned her head and hollered to no one in particular, "Hey, look at this! Calvin peed his pants!" She burst out guffawing, put her hand over her mouth as if to silence herself, and backed away gleefully.

Still staring and pointing, she shouted again, "Hey, did you see this?"

Calvin rose up out of the chair with a roar and with a closed fist hit her so hard she fell like a rock. Her head struck the edge of the mattress, she bounced to the floor and lay still.

"You dumb shit!" he screamed. I saw in Calvin's eyes, black as pitch, a mixture of shame and fear and murderous rage.

Tony and Wendell both dragged themselves from the bed and, as if in slow motion, came toward him. Calvin pounced, first on Tony who fell weakly to the floor, and then on Wendell, who, stronger and a bit more sober, managed to land a good punch to Calvin's midsection.

Calvin gasped and fell backward onto the floor next to the desk, quiet and spent. His head hung down, and his whole body shook with great, wrenching sobs.

"You goddamned son of a bitch," said Wendell. He turned, stepped over Pearl, who started to moan and writhe, jerked the door open, and left.

I stood as if frozen to the spot.

It rained the day we buried our father. We walked, a strangely solitary and pitiful little group, through wet prairie grass to the spot which had been excavated beside our mother's sunken mound, and we stood, shielded by a funeral canopy, as the preacher said the final words. The blonde sisters, children of Bonnie and Russell, sang "Whispering Hope" in two-part harmony as the casket was lowered into the dark grave, and I felt

Wendell beside me, his body rigid and trembling. When I turned to him and glared, barely able to stand his alcohol breath, I realized that he was stifling hysterical laughter. I punched him with my elbow, but he wouldn't be silenced.

"You know what they oughtta put on his tombstone?" he whispered in my ear.

"No, what?"

"He Beat His Dogs and His Kids." He held his arms out in front of him, measuring the length of the epitaph.

We turned away, holding on to each other, as Bonnie soulfully sprinkled a handful of dirt into the open grave.

The Cure

Mendoza was a little man; puny, you might say. But that was not the reason he took two Dilantin every day. Nor was it the reason that he carried with him quantities of multivitamins, which he ate like candy throughout the tedious days and sleepless nights. The puniness may have been the effect, rather than the cause. In any case, you noticed the smallness of the man right away. What you didn't notice at first was the other thing . . . the indefinable thing that made you forget about him as soon as he passed out of your field of vision. It was as though you saw him but that he wasn't really there amidst the bus passengers when you looked away, and it wasn't until your eyes fell upon him later that he became real.

That thing, whatever it was, Mendoza knew. And he tolerated it. Recently, he had become convinced that it had something to do with the doctors' telling him that he had the symptoms of Huntington's disease. Who the hell ever heard of that, he had wanted to ask when the Doc told him.

Well, Mr. Mendoza, it is inherited.

The hell?

Christ's sake! That's the shits, ennit...? Who would have thought that old Lakota woman who was his mother and that half-Mexican breed of a father would have passed this stuff on to him through faulty or diseased genes?

It turned out to be a "hell of a note," from Mendoza's point of view, for he just got smaller and punier, so, when he left the VA hospital, he vowed to really take care of himself. He even had a little booklet entitled *Amazing Grace,* which he read passages from every day. Stuff like this:

Abimelech, King of Gerar, had taken Abraham's wife as his own, but had done so innocently. Sarah was a beautiful woman and Abraham, fearful for his life, had said to Abimelech: "She is my sister." Indeed, Sarah, also fearful, had vouched for Abraham's life, telling the King "He is my brother."

Mendoza thought the story had something to do with failure and sin and guilt, and he kept reading it over and over. But he never really understood it. He knew that Sarah should be returned to her husband, and he feared incest as much as the next man. But he really couldn't figure it out. Still, he liked to read the story and think about it as he looked at the *Playboy* pictures he kept secreted between the pink shirt and green VA hospital pajamas in his suitcase.

Another part of taking good care of himself was making time to sit on his bed for a few minutes every night to sing from the little "*Children of Today*" booklet given to him by the Rev. C. F. Chadwick, Box 124, Bushnell, Nebraska. He sang a little song to the tune of "America":

> "Our blessed Christ so dear,
> May we to thee draw near.
> God bless each one.
> Lord, may we all be there.
> And for thee let us shine,
> God, save each one."

This was a part of the routine Mendoza had established for himself at the hospital, and, because he had some notion of how frail and tenuous his existence was, he sang the song on the all-night bus ride from Salt Lake City, Utah, to Pierre, South Dakota. You see, he couldn't take the chance of *not* singing it. The other passengers turned their heads and stared back at him, but it didn't matter. He kept up the singing until he felt satisfied that it was finished. The people on the bus saw his wild hair, his long gray coat, cheap and wrinkled. They thought he was drunk.

Mendoza was the last one off the bus when it stopped at the Capitol City, the Jewel of the Oahe Valley, Pierre, South Dakota, that cowboy and Indian town which was the last place on earth and the next place to Fort Thompson Agency of the Crow Creek Sioux. Mendoza thought that his footsteps echoed too loudly in the silent, dark night as he headed for the Locke Hotel, carrying his suitcase. But the echo was a good sound, not hollow as you might have thought.

He was home again. And already he knew it was going to be better this time. He was going to see Jerome and ask him to help make it right between himself and Belva. After all, it was no one's fault.

About a week later, Jerome's puzzled wife saw a suitcase on the sidewalk behind the house. She stopped and looked at it, wondering who had left it there. She carefully brought it into the house, opened it, and fingered the stiff collar of a pink shirt. Snapping the lid closed, she put the suitcase behind the door of the back bedroom. When she tried to talk to Jerome about it later, he showed no interest.

The next day, she took it to the basement.

The Clearest Blue Day

It is one of the strange contradictions in literature that pathos is something not ordinarily felt by the anguished; rather, it is felt by the observer, the spectator. Because this is so, I will tell you my story about a young Indian dancer, a black Christian missionary woman, and an old singer of the Wahpekute, all of whom I (as onlooker) characterize as significant figures in a changing Indian world. The three persons whom I have observed are fully engrossed in their lives, they are enormously compassionate, real and accomplished. And as composite players in a modern drama with historical undertones, they exemplify in their actions the other important contradiction in life, i.e., the more things change, the more they stay the same.

I

It was Sunday, the last day of *wacipi,* and this was the morning pause before the dancing resumed at noon.

Claude walked slowly from the camp through the brittle grass, past the temporary chemical toilets, and across the dirt road toward the nearly deserted dance arbor, where just the night before he had made it into the finals of the men's traditional dance contest. He still wore the red wraps of his dance outfit. He was drawn to the arbor by the sounds of a mellow bass voice, the clear vibrato of a lead guitar, and the sound of what his uncle Elgie used to call the "melody sax."

Only a few people were sitting in the shaded seats beneath the brilliant morning light, and without being very specific, Claude thought they looked like a sorry lot. There was a woman who looked about forty, her straight black hair oddly red-tinged, her brown hand covered with turquoise rings sweetly touching the trousers of her white-haired and goateed sixty-year-old companion. When her eyes unexpectedly met Claude's, she looked away as if unaccountably embarrassed. The white man sat with great dignity, his goatee as finely chiseled as his delicate face. Claude wondered if the woman was Ruth John's aunt, the one who had returned to the reservation after living in California for thirty years, the one who said that she was here to take care of her aged parents.

Near the microphone sat the white preacher, rigid with what Claude suspected was a pretense of appreciation, waiting for his time to address the skimpy audience. Earnest. Patient. With him, his pink-clad wife fussed over the stern-looking old lady at her side, their presences a sort of oblation of the religious present, and all of them, in Claude's mind at least, mere pathetic surrogates for the providential spirits of the land which Claude knew to be indigenous to this place.

Claude, the only young dancer present at this early morning Christian gathering, thought the music sounded a little raunchy for Sunday morning, but maybe he was in the mood for it. In any case, the music had invited him, so it seemed. It was rhythmic "Jesus comes" music in country-blues style, the sort of music that had gained much popularity on the reservation in recent times. The young dancer leaned his elbows on the cut-off poles that fenced in the arena and, drained and gaunt with loneliness, he listened to "Lord, What Can I Do?" songs, one right after the other.

As his eyes scanned the grounds, Claude watched baseball players from Little Wound, early for the game, lounge at the food stands, and later he couldn't take his gaze from the tall, slim Dakotah woman wearing sunglasses who strolled her baby on the curved rise of the entrance to the grounds. The baby stared straight ahead, and the woman eased herself and the stroller toward the camp area. She struck Claude as a particularly self-possessed young woman. It was in her walk, her long legs stretching and swaying, and, suddenly, he wished that he had married Julia and that such a baby as this was one that he might claim as his own and that he could see into the eyes of this anonymous woman and that she would smile.

This was the first dance in three years that Julia hadn't accompanied him, her enthusiasm for life, her innocent astonishment, her laughter which always transformed his natural gloom, her grace and sparkle gone. Today? Yesterday? When was it she told him, crying, that she could not stay? He had always known that she would someday leave him, and when she did, he acted off-hand, casual, as though life would go on as usual. Now, he leaned and listened, his sorrow profound, hidden.

Claude squinted into the sky. Then he looked out toward the water. In his early childhood days Claude had come to know every part of this river, every bend and turn, every fluvial characteristic of the land. He knew the places where the bank turned soft and treacherous, he knew how to anticipate the changing and shifting drop-offs as he swam, he knew where to catch the finest catfish. He had walked on the river's frozen surface in winter. But now the entire landscape was changed. There were no trees lining this river anymore. No wild plums turning ripe in July. No blue racers lying hidden in the brush. There were only vast blue man-made waters behind the hydropower dam near the Agency and powerboats on the waves. After the hydropower dams were constructed on this magnificent body of water, which even now continued to be fed by its tributaries, the river never froze over again in winter, and all things were changed irrevocably.

Claude's thoughts of Julia and his memories of the past seemed encased in cocoons made more brittle by what he began to see and understand as disasters of the modern world: hydropower dams flooding Indian land, stern fundamentalist preachers taking the place of the Catholic Fathers, church guitars and country singers belting out religious songs. And Julia. And Julia.

The sky sparkled just a bit and the whitecaps on the vast expanse of water started to billow and swell and the wind rose. It was the clearest blue day.

II

"Where the ro-o-o-ses never fade," sang the serene girl in the black porkpie hat, her black skin gleaming, as shiny as the tight black leatherlike slacks she wore. She stood between the long-haired, unkempt-looking Indian sax player and the lead guitarist, and her left foot tapped out the rhythm ever so softly. As newcomers straggled in the empty arbor, she left the trio and picked up Christian songbooks and walked spiritlessly across to each newcomer to hand him or her a hymnal. As she passed Claude, she held one out to him, but he turned a shoulder to her and pretended an interest in the horizon.

"Come to the Lord, where the ro-o-o-oses never fade," she mouthed, her voice scarcely a whisper. She felt a sudden monumental emptiness that made it difficult for her to go on. Nonetheless, she rejoined the group at the microphone and once again looked her companions-in-song full in the face and began to welcome the clear blue day that she had chosen to give to Jesus. She watched the young Indian dancer as he stared at a woman in sunglasses placidly strolling her baby across the grounds, and she put her head down, closed her eyes, and sang with renewed fervor.

She remembered now. Her sanguine expectations as she reached for the telephone that night in Albuquerque had turned to relief when she heard that her assignment in missionary work was to be on a Northern Plains Indian reservation. She had always wanted to work with Indians, even though she recognized that in such cases where poverty was rampant, sacrifice and virtue in the name of God's work might go unappreciated. Her belief was that she was significantly inspired and dedicated, and she could rise above any obstacles.

"American Indians are the needliest of all God's creatures," Reverend told her, "and now that you are finished with your divinity training, you can offer yourself to them and to Jesus." She was ready.

She had audaciously and hurriedly packed her Toyota with her few belongings. She had driven almost straight north out of New Mexico, finally making her way through endless prairie grasslands, until she'd caught sight of the largest body of water she'd seen in several days of travel, the new Missouri River in all its splendor formed into a huge lake at the head of a large hydropower dam, one of several such sights along its vast length.

"It's beautiful!" she had exclaimed to no one in particular.

Throughout the months and years that followed, the memory of that moment never dimmed in the mind of the young woman, in spite of the harsh realities of Christian missionary life on the reservation in the modern world. Sadly, her own personal enthusiasm eventually turned into a quiet despair.

"There is not the ready acceptance of the Lord's teachings that I had envisioned," she told the Reverend, who telephoned her from his Utah headquarters for bimonthly reports.

"What do you mean?" he asked.

"Well, they come if we've got something to give the children, like food or gifts. But, otherwise, they seem uninterested."

"Reverend Thompson seems very unhappy here," she went on, "and his wife and mother-in-law just stay in the house all the time."

"Don't be discouraged," she was told over and over again.

She didn't confide in her mentor that she found herself bored with the lives that these people lived and that it had become a remarkable fact that she seldom talked to them about Jesus and his compassion and wisdom anymore. Rather, she had begun talking endlessly about herself to anyone who would listen, told stories about her own childhood near Carlsbad, growing up black in New Mexico, and how she had been poor and how her mother had deserted the family of seven children.

And now it was Sunday, the last day of *wacipi*.

"Turn to page seventy-three," the young black woman said into the microphone, her voice suddenly hollow and impersonal.

Diminishing the other sounds, her voice rang into the clear blue day. "Where could I go but to the Lord?" she sang.

III

The old man sat alone in the sun. Exclusive. Solitary.

His gray hair was loose, and it hung untidily over

his shoulders under a battered, aged, and unadorned Stetson. He wore mustard-colored cowboy boots, one heel keeping time to the gospel music. His face was one of those faces that one sees in photographic extravaganzas, an expression of the classic image of American Indians, his bronzed hauteur somehow out of place at this pathetic gathering of Christians, his unposed and incongruous presence a tribute to the survival of a people assaulted for centuries by a confused mixture of racial hatred and good intentions.

He accepted the hymnal thrust into his hands by the young black woman in shiny slacks, and then he leaned forward with his elbows on his knees and silently followed along on all of the songs that were sung throughout the morning. Every now and then he lowered his head and closed his eyes wearily and swayed imperceptibly to the rhythm of the music.

This was the last day of *wacipi* and the old man, a renowned traditional singer and dancer of the Wahpekute, was tired. During the previous two days he had carried the eagle-feather flag for the opening ceremonies, and he had danced almost without interruption, and later, when he had given the communal prayer, he had sung a very old song of courage that his grandfather had taught him, a song that had not been heard for fifty years in such a public gathering as this. Today he was tired, and he sat resting, listening easily to the Christian hymns, the thumping of the guitar and saxophone, and he felt vaguely happy.

Behind the old man the whitecaps on the gray-blue waters flashed and dipped. The sun blazed, and it was the clearest blue day.

IV

Corporeal, substantial, rhythmic, the long line of dancers streamed into the arbor, making its way slowly and inexorably toward the East to form the Sacred Circle.

Like a large, natural flow of water, the dancers representing the People, the Dakotapi, poured into the dance arbor, each one brilliantly painted and adorned, carefully stepping in time to the drum, heeding the heartbeats of their own humanity and the humanity of all generations.

The weary old man had abandoned the Stetson and the yellow cowboy boots, and now, showing no signs of fatigue, he followed the flags, his body shaking with intense and animated preoccupation with the dance. He was resplendent in porcupine hair, quills, eagle feathers, and beaded regalia. His crouched stance and the tilt of his head carefully imitated the dance of his ancestors, whose feet had touched this sacred ground as long ago as memory and imagination could distinguish.

Youthful male dancers moved in and out of the line like feeding and discharging tributaries, converging and separating along the course of the movement of the major stream. Traditional female dancers, lustrous in buckskin and shell and bone and beads, like the flashing and dipping waves of the river in the distance, emerged into the noon sun, stately symbols of fidelity and truth.

Claude felt the drumbeats, and his eyes, shaded by sunglasses, glistened. Tall and disdainful, his forehead painted crimson, he was absorbed in the motion and sounds of the processional. He had forgotten Julia. He had forgotten the disasters of the modern world. He was dancing as his grandfathers had danced in the sun, and it was the clearest blue day. The hills in the distance were white and brown and green. Claude closed his eyes momentarily, and he knew that the hills were there and they cradled the terrible river in accordance with some reasonable and primeval order. His feet touched the earth in time with the drum, in harmony with his heartbeat, in time with history and the present and his heartbeat. He danced with the others, and in so doing, he drew the hills and the river and the People into one entity. He and the others came here this blue day to do this thing as had been done always by the People.

The young black woman, her arms full of Christian hymnals recently gathered up from the brief Christian service held in this arbor, stood casually and tiredly at the opposite entrance. She paid scant attention to the ceremonial entrance of the dancers into the arbor, distracted by the rising wind which blew dust around her legs and into her eyes. She drew a scarf around her head to hold the porkpie hat securely, and then she turned and walked slowly to her car.

The Power of Horses

The mother and daughter steadied themselves, feet planted squarely, foreheads glistening with perspiration, and each grasped a handle of the large, steaming kettle.

"Ready?"

"Un-huh."

"Take it, then," the mother said. "Careful." Together they lifted the tub of boiled beets from the flame of the burners on the gas stove and set it heavily on the table across the room. The girl let the towel which had served as a makeshift pot holder drop to the floor as the heat penetrated to the skin, and she slapped her hand against the coolness of the smooth, painted wall and then against her thigh, feeling the roughness of the heavy jeans with tingling fingers. To stop the tingling, she cupped her fingers to her mouth and blew on them, then raised her apologetic eyes and looked at her mother. Without speaking, as if that was the end of it, she sank into the chrome chair and picked up the towel and began wiping the sweat from her face. The sun came relentlessly through the thin gauze curtains, and the hot wind blew gently across the stove, almost extinguishing the gas flames of the burners, making the blue edges turn yellow and then orange and then white. The towel was damp now and stained purple from the beets, and the girl leaned back in the chair and laid the towel across her face, feeling her own hot breath around her nose and mouth.

"Your hands get used to it, Marleen," the mother said, not even glancing at the girl, nor at her own rough, brown hands, "just have to keep at it," saying this not so much from believing it as from the need to stop this feeling of futility in the girl and the silence between them. The mother gingerly grasped the bleached stems of several beets and dropped them into a pan of cold water, rolling one and then another of the beets like balls in her hands, pushing the purple-black skins this way and that, quickly, deftly removing the peel and stem and tossing the shiny vegetable into another container. Finishing one, she hurriedly picked up another, as if by hurrying she could forestall the girl's rebellion.

The woman's arms, like her hands, were large, powerful. But, despite the years of heavy work, her sloping shoulders and smooth, long neck were part of a tender femininity only recently showing small signs of decline and age. The dark stains on her dark face might have seemed like age spots or a disfigurement on someone else, but on the woman they spread delicately across her cheeks, forehead, and neck like a sweep of darkened cloud, making her somehow vulnerable and defenseless.

"Your hands'll get used to it, Marleen," she repeated, again attempting to keep the girl's unwillingness in check, and an avenue to reasonable tolerance and cooperation open.

The brief rest with the towel on her face seemed to diminish the girl's weariness, and for an instant more she sat silently, breathing peacefully into the damp towel. As the girl drew the towel across her face and away from her eyes, something like fear began to rise in her, and she peered out the window, where she saw her father standing with a white man she had never seen before. Her father was looking straight ahead down the draw where the horses stood near the corral. They always want something from him, she thought, and as she watched the white man put a cigarette in his mouth and turn sideways out of the wind, the flame of his lighter licking toward his bony profile, she wondered what it was this time. She watched the man's quick mannerisms, and she saw that he began to talk earnestly and gesture toward his green pickup truck, which was parked close to the barbed-wire fence encircling the house and yard.

The girl was startled out of her musings at the sound of her mother's "*yu-u-u-u,*" the softly uttered indication of disapproval, insistent, always compelling a change in the girl's behavior. And she turned quickly to get started with her share of the hot beets, handling them inexpertly, but peeling their hot skins away as best she could. After a few minutes, during which the women worked in silence, only the monotonous hiss of the burning gas flame between them, the girl, surprised, thought: her sounds of disapproval aren't because I'm wasting time; instead, they are made because she is afraid my father and the white man will see me watching them. Spontaneously, defensively, she said, "They didn't see me." She looked into the brown-stained face but saw only her mother's careful pretense of being preoccupied with the beets, as she picked up a small knife to begin slicing them. All last winter, every time I came home, I spied on him for you, thought the girl, even riding my horse over to Chekpa's through the snow to see if he was there. And when I came back and told you that he was, you acted as if you hadn't heard anything, like now. So this is not the beginning of the story, nor is it the part of the story that matters, probably, thought the girl, and she started to recognize a long, long history of acrimony between her parents, thinking, in hindsight, that it would have been better if she had stayed at Stephen Mission. But then, she remembered her last talk with Brother Otto at the Mission as he sat before her, one leg languidly draped over the other, his collar open, showing his sparse red chest hairs, his watery, pale eyes looking at her searchingly, and she knew that it wasn't better to have stayed there.

He had sat quivering with sympathy as she had tried to tell him that to go home was to be used by her mother against her father. I rode over to Chekpa's, she told him, hating herself that she was letting out the symptoms of her childish grief, despising him for his delicate white skin, his rapt gaze, the vicariousness of his measly existence, and *Até* was there, cutting wood for the eldest of the Tatiopa women, Rosalie, the one he was supposed to marry, you know, but, instead, he married my mother. My mother sent me there, and when I rode into the yard and saw him, he stood in uncertainty, humiliated in the eyes of Chekpa, his old friend, as well as all of those in the Tatiopa family. Worse yet, she knew, humiliated in the eyes of his nine-year-old daughter.

In her memory of that awful moment, she didn't speak, nor did her father, and so she had ridden out of the yard as abruptly as she had come and home at a dead gallop, standing easily in the stirrups, her face turned toward her right shoulder out of the wind, watching the slush fly behind the horse's hooves. She didn't cut across Archie's field as she usually did, but took the long way, riding as hard as she could alongside the road. When she got to the gate she reined in, dismounted, and led her horse through the gate and then, slowly, down the sloping hill to the tack shed. She stood for a long time with her head against the wide, smooth leather of the stirrup shaft, her eyes closed tightly and the smell of wet horse hair in her nostrils. Much later she had recited the event as fully as she could bear to the mission school priest, much as she had been taught to recite the events of her sinful life: I have taken the Lord's name in vain, I have taken the Lord's name in vain, I have tak . . .

Damn beets, damn all these damn beets, the girl

thought, and she turned away from the table back to the stove, where she stirred the second, smaller, pot of sliced beets, and she looked out through the gauze curtains to see if her father and the white man were still there. They had just run the horses into the corral from the small fenced pasture where they usually grazed when they were brought down to the place.

"He must be getting ready to sell them, is he?" she asked her mother.

Her mother said nothing.

"How come? I didn't know he was going to sell," the girl said slowly, noticing that her horse, two quarter-horse brood mares, and a half-Shetland black-and-white gelding she had always called "*Shōta*" had been cut out of the herd and were standing at the far corner of the pasture, grazing. The heat shimmered above the long buffalo grass, and the girl's thoughts drifted, and, vaguely, she heard her mother say, "You'd better spoon those sliced ones into these hot jars, Marleen," and then, almost to herself, her mother started talking as if in recognition of what the girl did not know about the factual and philosophical sources from which present life emerges. "I used to have land, myself, daughter," she began, "and on it my grandfather had many horses. What happened to it was that some white men from Washington came and took it away from me when my grandfather died because, they said, they were going to breed game birds there; geese, I think.

"There was no one to do anything about it," she continued, "there was only this old woman who was a mother to me, and she really didn't know what to do, who to see, or how to prevent this from happening.

"Among the horses there on my land was a pair of brood mares just like those two out there." She pointed with her chin to the two bays at the end of the pasture. And, looking at the black-and-white horse called *Shōta*, she said, "And there was also another strange, mysterious horse, *su'ka wak a'*," *i-e-e-e*, she had used the word for "mysterious dog" in the Dakotah language. And the mother and daughter stood looking out the window at the the *shōta* horse beside the bays, watching them pick their way through the shimmering heat and through the tall grass, slowly, unhurried. The beets were forgotten, momentarily, and the aging woman remembered the magic of those horses and especially the one that resembled the *shōta* horse, thinking about that time, that primordial time when an old couple of the tribe received a gift horse from a little bird, and the horse produced many offspring for the old man and woman, and the people were never poor after that. Her grandfather, old Bowed Head, the man with many horses, had told her that story often during her childhood when he wished to speak of those days when all creatures knew one another . . . and it was a reassuring thing. "I wish this tribe to be strong and good," the mysterious horse had told the old man, "and so I keep giving my offspring every year and the tribe will have many horses and this good thing will be among you always."

"They were really fast horses," said the mother, musing still, filling in the texture of her imagination and memory, "they were known throughout our country for their speed, and the old man allowed worthy men in the tribe to use them in war or to go on a hunt with them. It is an old story," the woman concluded, as though the story were finished, as though commenting upon its history made everything comprehensible.

As the girl watched her mother's extraordinary vitality, which rose during the telling of these events, she also noted the abruptness with which the story seemed to end and the kind of formidable reserve and closure which fell upon the dark, stained features as the older woman turned again to the stove.

"What happened to the horses?" the girl wanted to know. "Did someone steal them? Did they die?"

After a long silence her mother said, "Yes, I suppose so," and the silence again deepened between them as they fell to filling hot jars with sliced beets and sealing hot lids upon them, wiping and stroking them meticulously and setting them one by one on a dim pantry shelf.

The girl's frustration was gone now, and she seemed mindless of the heat, her own physical discomfort, and the miserableness of the small, squalid kitchen where she and her mother moved quietly about, informed now with the wonder of the past, the awesomeness of the imagination.

The sun moved west and the kitchen fell into shadow, the wind died down, and the mother and daughter finished their tedious task and carried the large tub of hot water out through the entryway a few feet from the door and emptied its contents upon the ground. The girl watched the red beet juice stain the dry, parched earth in which there was no resistance, and she stepped away from the redness of the water, which gushed like strokes of a painter's brush, suddenly black and ominous, as it sank into the ground. She looked up to see the white man's green pickup truck disappear over the rise, the dust billowing behind the heavy wheels, settling gently in the heat.

The nameless fear struck at her again and she felt a knot being drawn tightly inside her and she looked anxiously toward the corral. Nothing around her seemed to be moving, the air suddenly still, the sweat standing out in beads on her face and her hands, oddly, moist and cold. As she ran toward the corral, she saw her mother out of the corner of her eye, still grasping one handle of the boiler tub, strangely composed, her head and shoulders radiant in the sun.

At the corral, moments later, she saw her father's nearly lifeless form lying facedown in the dirt, his long gray hair spread out like a fan above him, pitifully untidy for a man who ordinarily took meticulous care with his appearance. He had his blue cotton scarf which he used as a handkerchief clutched tightly in his right hand, and he was moaning softly.

The odor of whiskey on his breath was strong as she helped him turn over and sit up, and in that instant the silent presence of the past lay monumentally between them, so that he did not look at her nor did he speak.

In that instant she dimly perceived her own innocence and was filled with regret that she would never know those times to which *Até* would return, if he could, again and again. She watched as he walked unsteadily toward the house, rumpled and drunk, a man of grave dignity made comic and sad and helpless by circumstances which his daughter could only regard with wonderment.

Keyapi: Late one night, when the old man had tied the horses near his lodge, someone crept through the draw and made ready to steal them; it was even said that they wanted to kill the wonderful horses. The mysterious gift horse called to the sleeping old man and told him that an evil lurked nearby. And he told the old man that since such a threat as this had come upon them and all the people of the tribe, the power of the horses would be diminished, and no more colts would be born and the people would have to go back to their miserable ways.

As her father made his way to the house, walking stiffly past her mother, who pretended to be scrubbing the black residue from the boiler, the girl turned and walked quickly away from the corral in the opposite direction.

I must look: she thought, into the distance, and as she lifted her eyes and squinted into the evening light, she saw the Fort George road across the river, beyond the bend in the river, so far away that it would take most of the day for anyone to get there from where she walked. I must look: at the ground in front of me where my grandmothers made paths to the ti(n)psina beds and carried home with them long braided strands over their shoulders. I must look: she thought, into the past for the horse that speaks to humans.

She took long strides and walked into the deepening dusk. She walked for a long time before returning to the darkened house, where she crept into her bed and lay listening to the summer's night insect sounds, thinking apocalyptic thoughts in regard to what her mother's horse story might have to do with the day's events.

She awoke with a start, her father shaking her shoulder. "You must ride with me today, daughter, before the horse buyer comes back," he said. "I wish to take the horses way out to the far side of the north pasture. I am ready to go, so please hurry."

The girl dressed quickly, and just as dawn was breaking, she and her father, each leading two horses, with the others following, set out over the prairie hills. These were the hills, she knew, to which the people had come when the Uprising was finished and the U.S. Cavalry fell to arguing with missionaries and settlers about the "Indian problem." These were the hills, dark blue in this morning light, which she knew as repositories of sacred worlds unknown to all but its most ancient tenants.

When they reached the ridge above Dry Creek, the girl and her father stopped and let the horses go their way, wildly. The *shōta* horse led them down the steep prairie hills and into the dry creek bed and, one by one, the horses of the herd disappeared into the stand of heavy cottonwood trees which lined the ravine.

She stood beside her father and watched them go. "Why were you going to sell them?" she asked abruptly.

"There are too many," he replied, "and the grass is short this summer. It's been too hot," he said, wiping his face with the blue handkerchief, and he repeated, "The grass is short this summer."

With that, they mounted their horses and rode home together.

Going Home

He remembered the rain. The goddamned rain. When he left Saigon it had been raining for five, six weeks. And it was still raining on the Dakota Plains when he got there a few days later.

"Don't you like that story, Young Nephew?" The Little Nun, her cheeks rosy and round, beamed at him. "Odysseus has at last come home, hasn't he?"

"Yeah."

"And while the maid washes his feet, he has to hide the scar from her."

"Yeah."

"So they won't know who he is, don't you see?"

"Uh-hunmh."

He was just six years old when the Little Nun read the story to him. It was then that she taught him how to read and write, and in the subsequent years he had become a voracious reader. He loved to read, preferring it to sports and games. Later, the Little Nun taught him algebra and he got so good at it that he could beat every- one in class at solving problems.

As he walked across the deserted street from the gas station where they were trying to fix his car, he stepped over the puddles at the curb and looked up at the threat- ening sky, distant and discolored.

This had always been a wide-open town, and the Sioux who had traded here with the white men since the 1700s, when Frenchmen like Charles Pierre LeSeuer and others came here in search of furs, knew it better than most. The Verendrye brothers, they say, came here and claimed much of this territory for France.

Young Nephew smiled. They could make whatever claims they wanted, he thought, but the Sioux, for longer than anyone could know, had always come home from war to places like this. Unlike the Frenchmen, Young Nephew needed to make no claims. But, like the Greek epic warrior, he knew that he was coming in se- cret, hiding the scar that had everything to do with who he was.

Prior to white settlement, great Sioux encampments were often staged on the flat prairie above this now ragged town. Every spring the tribes performed incan- descent ceremonials to renew alliances and maintain the peace or make war plans or welcome warriors back from the paths of war or exchange goods and renew old acquaintances. Ah, there's no ceremonials this spring, thought Young Nephew regretfully as he walked down the street, his boots echoing on the pavement.

His grandfather had run two hundred head of horses there along the Missouri River. His people knew that they had taken in that prairie river country of the Northern Plains, absorbed it into their hearts and minds and never lost their longing for its love.

"No matter how distant and absent you are," his grandmother had often told him when he was a little boy at her knee, "you will always be destined for recognition by this land. It will never forget you."

He was not the first modern warrior to return in this way. His father in 1919, not as a citizen of the United States, but as a warrior of the Sioux nation, returned from a tour of World War I duty in Europe, and Young Nephew had heard his story of homecoming many times.

"When I got back to South Dakota from Chicago in 1919," his father would say with a smile when he was in the mood to reminisce, *"I was still wearing my uniform, and I waited for two days at the train station in Chamberlain for my youngest brother, Lawrence, to come and get me. From* kudwichacha."

It was a mythical story. But the old man always laughed out loud and cursed as he told it.

*"And then here he come, riding a bay mare and leading
a second horse." With great enthusiasm he would con-
clude, "And I never hardly left the Crow Creek again.
God damn!" he would say softly, after a final pause, "if
he hadn't come I was gonna get back on that train, leave
forever, and never come back. It looked pretty bad
around here then, you know. It was before the Reorganization Act, and it was when they had still outlawed
our sun dance." Smiling, still, he would recall, "But
there he was and he had that old gelding I broke to ride
when I was just a kid. And that hand-tooled saddle my
uncle give me. And my Mexican silver spurs was tied to
the saddle horn. And I knew I was home."*

Yeah, *Até*, all roads lead home, Young Nephew
thought at the time. That was that border town, Chamberlain. 1919. This is Fort Pierre. Fifty years later. And
there's not a hell of a lot of difference. Except that I just
drove in from Salt Lake City and my fan belt's broke.
Damn near didn't make it at all.

And now. We start again. The old man's health was
bad and he, Young Nephew, would work with his
brothers to salvage what they could. The ranch lands
waited. We won't give it up, *Até*.

*Those roads of hard-packed earth streaked with the
    familiarity of noon sag where heat-struck reptiles
    smear their unborn
    and dogs live out the defeat of their own silence*

soft, warm old women ignore my thin embrace
Those roads to the wombs of the sovereign tribes
   motherlands to starvelings
   born again by taking the veil,
   entering religious orders,
   reciting cantos to the Holy Ghost
Those roads that pass the recent profligate
   Missouri
   that process server for Jefferson who only wanted
   to replace the Indian Head Nickel
   and set up residence anywhere in the darkness
   of the cave
Those roads that pass the graveyards
Those roads that pass by the severely wounded
   come, finally, to the place where I grew up by
   the campfires
   snuffed out by colonials who brought with
   them
   the frame houses with closed porches
   jogging suits
   Black Hills Power and Light
   Valedictorians
   And Pied Pipers of every order

He walked carelessly along the street with a confi-
dence in his stride that indicated a kind of aimlessness,
and if he had thought about it at all, he would have
recognized in his own physical attitude a painful at-
tempt to divorce himself from the present. He turned

abruptly into the Silver Spur. He still wore the khaki-colored T-shirt of his military service and felt in the pockets of his green/gray fatigues for some change. He stood for a moment to let his eyes adjust to the darkness of the lounge and listened to what he had always called "cowboy music," the familiar whine about lost love and inevitable regret. With some sarcasm, he thought, That's what I'm needin', ennit? Cheer up, fella. As his eyes adjusted to the dim lighting of the smoke-filled room, he saw an old friend seated at the bar.

"*Koda.*" He touched the man's shoulder.

Laroche showed no great surprise as they shook hands, and it was as if they had seen each other just last week. Could it be, thought Young Nephew, that I've not killed a dozen men since I saw him last? That I didn't run around some jungle for weeks on end without changing my socks? Is this real? Could it be that I haven't gone to hell and back and wept that I'd never see my home again? Naw! I'm not a hundred years old! Everything's just like it used to be! Sure!

"*Hau!*" said Laroche. "Hey, Big Pipe," calling him by his family name, "*toke' he' niye'.* So? Is it you?"

"Yeah . . . *hau!*"

"*Tuktel he?*" "Where have you been?"

Young Nephew shrugged, reluctant at first. "Just got here."

"What's new?"

"Nuthin'. Just drove in from Salt Lake."

"Yeah?"

"Well, more recently, from Saigon," Young Nephew said with a brittle laugh.

After that offhand admission he felt ordinary again, no need to play a role. As though just saying it out loud transposed his own modern version of the return of Odysseus upon his father's *kudwichacha* homecoming story and gave chronology to the presence of shifting death scenes which flashed in his memory. It made these memories seem like ordinary human celebrations which occur because one is lucky enough to escape the appalling disintegration brought about by war. He thought for just an instant, *'iya ma c'eca.* . . . I am like him, my father, or that Greek hero. And it doesn't matter that I must compare my life to perfection, because I know that historical perspectives are merely fragmentary.

He was therefore surprised when Laroche took his arm and said, "Jesus, let me buy you a drink."

They sat comfortably in silence, until a blonde woman came in, put a friendly arm around Laroche, and ordered a drink.

"*Tuwe* . . ." Young Nephew pointed with his chin.

"Oh, let me introduce you to Sandi," said Laroche, as though he just remembered. "Sandi Nelson. You know, Craig's wife . . . Craig Nelson?"

No, he didn't know Craig Nelson. Someone he had forgotten, perhaps. But it didn't matter.

They reached across the bar to shake hands. She smiled.

"Hey, you wanna dance?"

"Sure."

She jumped up and stuffed out her cigarette. She walked past him to the tiny, dingy dance floor, turned, and lifted her arms. She was very sure of herself and looked into his eyes as her hips began to twist. He moved his feet slowly and circled her.

"Come now, honey . . . ," she said, motioning. "I been just waitin' for you."

Out of the corner of his eye he saw a smirk on Laroche's dark face, and he wondered what the joke was.

He pulled her close and said slowly, "Well, waitin's half the fun."

She was skinny and nearly as tall as he, a small-breasted woman with freckles on her otherwise pale arms. Her shoulder-length hair was straight and bleached, and her jeans were skintight. For the first time in weeks, Young Nephew relaxed. To hell with the rain, he thought. To hell with my goddamned fan belt. He closed his eyes and felt her skinny thighs against him.

There was something about her.

But just as quickly the skinny blonde faded away and he saw the mirror of his own darkened eyes glittering in the refracted jungle light and they were filled with tears.

He tightened his arms around the blonde, and just as he was about to let her turn, he heard an angry voice at his shoulder.

"You goddamned whore!"

The blonde stiffened, and Young Nephew heard her whisper, "Oh, shit! That's Craig."

When he looked at her blankly, she said, "My husband . . ."

Young Nephew was laughing as he turned. "Hey, man. It's okay. I don't mean . . ."

Craig's right jab grazed his ear, feebly and with no great enthusiasm. But it was enough to make Young Nephew instantly angry, and, with a groan, he knocked the aggrieved husband to the floor.

As though Young Nephew were no longer even there, the husband jumped up and let go with an ear-splitting verbal rage directed toward his now trembling wife.

"You slut!" he screamed, saliva spewing from his lips.

She stared.

"What you doin' with him?" He jerked his thumb toward Young Nephew.

The blood rose in her face as her husband reached for her arms and pulled her toward the chairs. She tried to back away.

People in the bar watched with mild interest.

"You gotta go fuckin' around with Indians, you're worse off'n I thought!"

He slapped her hard enough to cut her lip, which she covered quickly with her hand.

Young Nephew grabbed the man by the throat, knocked him to the floor again, and started choking him. He wouldn't let go until Laroche pounded on him, hollering, "Hey, you're gonna kill him! Let him go! Let him go!" Young Nephew released his grip, and the man rushed out the door, his wife close behind.

"Hey, you better knock it off, Pipe," Laroche admonished. "They'll throw us outta here."

"Well," Young Nephew said, rubbing an elbow he'd scraped in the fracas, "I've got throwed outta better places.

"That white son of a bitch," he said, throwing one leg over the stool. "Did you see that white man . . . that goddamned *wasichu?*"

"Yeah?" said Laroche sarcastically, disgusted now with this unnecessary brawl. "So he's a white man. So what? You don't think you come home from Saigon to rid the world of white men, do you?" He returned to his bar stool and grabbed his beer.

Still fuming, but beginning to see the humor in the little scuffle, Young Nephew started to laugh.

"The world? The *world?* Who the hell cares about the world? Hell, I had enough of the goddamned world! Just get 'em outta Sioux country, hunh?"

Roaring now with laughter, the two men turned their attention to the bar, and Laroche ordered again.

Young Nephew turned away and downed his drink, hoping no one would see his shaking hands.

"I gotta go see about my car," he said and left suddenly, Laroche staring after him.

Outside, the rain had turned into a downpour, and

as he ran across the street, his tears streamed down his face.

For now he had to hide what he knew to be fact, that he would have choked a man to death without a moment's hesitation if Laroche hadn't been there to pull him away. Young Nephew was home from the Asian War.

Flight

Facing up to it. That's how Velma thought about her mother's impending death. *God, how I hate to face up to it. What is the point of this agony?* For two years now the old woman has been near death, rallying, weakening, resisting, and constantly asking someone for a way out. The last time I visited her, I heard her voice from the entrance down the hall: "Help me! Help! Help me!" When I got to her side, I said, *"Ee-enah!* What are you hollering for? You stop that," and she looked at me vacantly, hollow-eyed and desperate, her shoulders bent forward in her wheelchair. Convulsively, her body shook as she cried out: "Help! Help!"

God, how I hate to face up to it.

She looked out of the window, felt the big jet rock back and forth gently. She felt dizzy. The stewardess slammed the lid down on the overhead rack just in front of her, and Velma's ears felt a sharp jab. Irritably she pressed her head against the seat cushion and stared resolutely ahead at the Fly Free sign posted above the Exit light. Momentarily distracted, she thought, Am I the only one who understands irony? Or is that sort of thing now called black humor?

She had been in constant touch with the young white man social worker whose office was across the hall from her mother's room. "If the worst happens," he had asked during the last telephone conversation, "which funeral home shall I call?"

I wonder what do you mean, "the worst," Mark? To die is not the worst that one can do, and the old woman has lived a good life. Do you mean that she may die before I get there? Would that be "the worst"? But I saw her only last week. After her bath she lay in bed on her side, and her convulsive call for help had stopped as mysteriously as it had started. I held her hand, looked into her clouded eyes, and knew that the business of Hell and Heaven and Satan and Sin was not on our minds. "Where are my dishes?" she had asked. "The ivory-colored ones with pink flowers? Where are they?" The question pierced my soul.

She felt the movement of the huge jet backing slowly away from the boarding platform as the stewardess's nasal voice came over the intercom. "This is flight one six seven two, seven thirty-seven service to Salt Lake City."

Lights blinked.

On the runway below, a small tractor pulled a huge

Alaska Airlines jet down the slick path, a ludicrous Promethean spectacle of modern technology.

She felt the pressure as she was lifted into the sky, the rumble of the landing gear. The clouds closed around her, and she knew she was going to die. She felt a wave of panic, and her heart thudded in her ears. Suddenly, the orange and blue and gray sunset flared in the window. Below, the shadowed, frozen earth lay silent as the darkened pressurized cabin enveloped her, hissing. Her ears bubbled.

"I'll be there, Mark," she had shouted into the telephone. "Wait! Make her wait!"

She felt a tightness in her chest as she watched the blonde stewardess leaning over a middle-aged man in first class, stretching her lacquered mouth into what was designed to be a wide, flashing invitation.

Why didn't I go home at Christmastime . . . ? Why did I . . . ? Why . . . ? It happened the same way when *Até* died. And I wasn't there . . . Why didn't I go . . . Why wasn't I there?

The setting sun was all of a sudden a liquid band of fire on the horizon, so bright that she had to squint her eyes as she faced the flaming orange glow. Red. Gold. Above the cemented clouds.

I just want her to look at me again and know that I came. That's all. Just if she can see me. She will know me. Tell her to WAIT!

A dark and diffused cloud cover moved across the streak of flame on the horizon, and afterwards, all that was left was the light blue of the night sky, wisps of gray puffs blurring the clean line of the horizon like puffy, sparse hairs on an otherwise smooth surface.

I want to tell her . . . I want to tell her . . .

Tears filled her eyes as she looked at the monitor in the busy terminal. Flight 3882. On Time. She blew her nose and stuffed her handkerchief into her purse as she hurried to make her connection.

A Firm and Continuous Desire

*...the firm and continuous desire to render to
everyone that which is his due...*
JUSTINIAN

I

Ed saw Jennee watching as he brought his horse closer
to the porch, dismounted, and walked past her into the
room where he kept his 30-30 standing behind the door.
"*Tokiya la he?*" she asked. "Where are you going?"
Without answer or comment he picked up his gun
and walked back outside, put his foot in the stirrup, and
lifted himself gracefully into the saddle. With a slight,
quick pressure of his heels into the flank of the old buckskin gelding, he set out at an easy gait for the Joe Creek,
which wound its way through his mother's allotment
and emptied into the Missouri River. Edmund had always thought of it as an extraordinary creek, one which
faithfully brought moisture to the dry, windswept hills,

no matter how little rain came. Now he kept thirty-five heifers ready to calve and some old cows along its soft banks. The water was sweet and clear.

It was eight miles to the Joe Creek from Ed's place, not a long ride, but a demanding one under the sun's heat. When he got there, Ed noticed that his horse was lathered and breathing hard, so he tied him to the far fence, away from the water. Then he grasped the steel barrel of the rifle from its saddle shaft, checked the ammunition, and, with elbows held high and away from his body, he jogged lightly and purposefully to the moist creek bank, which sloped gently down to the water. There! He saw the fifteen sows sloshing at the banks, grunting and snorting, wallowing in mud up to their bellies. He took careful aim on the fattest of them, and as she looked up dully, he pulled the trigger. The fat sow sank into the creek, blood oozing from her snout. Methodically and quickly, Ed shot them all. Then he untied his horse, now quivering and nervous from the shots, and led him upstream a quarter of a mile to drink from the cool, refreshing water. He mounted his horse and rode home.

"It is my land that the squaw man uses for his pigs," he told Jennee later as he pulled off his boots and got ready for bed, "my mother's allotment."

When the frightened Bureau of Indian Affairs range man questioned him about the incident the next day, Ed said, "I told him that my cattle and horses don't like to drink at the same place the pigs drink. It may be that he is deaf." Ed eventually paid for the slaughtered pigs. He and the squaw man never spoke another word between them.

II

Alive, Edmund Big Pipe was a symbol, a thinker, a constant; dead he was no less so. He had been considered a troublemaker by the reservation officials from the time his mother gave breath to him in a *tipi* ten miles south of old agency, Sisseton, South Dakota, to the time some eighty-eight years later when he fainted and expired on the banks of the Missouri near Iron Nation. Just at that last moment of his life, the old man's lips pursed and his lower jaw opened as though he had some final statement, but he couldn't speak. His wife knelt beside him and closed the gaping mouth and staring eyes with trembling fingers.

Jennee managed to lift his inert, frail body into the Dodge truck. She picked up the string of smooth fish he had just caught that afternoon, and she drove to the two-room house where she had lived with him for nearly sixty years. She called her daughter, who lived fifteen hundred miles away. "He is dead," she said into the telephone.

III

The funeral which followed Ed's death was a long and ceremonious affair: his daughter sang of grief and loss

in the old traditional way of women; many songs of
honor were sung by groups from Four Agencies; and
long speeches, emotional and compelling, were given in
the archaic language of the ancestors. Vilas Knife, desolate and anguished, led the Dakotah singers in the
Christian dirge "Eventide," in carefully enunciated, ancient and measured sounds, never raising his eyes from
the hymnal he shared with the others:

Wa-kan-tan-ka kin o-wan-ca-ya un, Is-na-na hin
o-wa-sin sdon-ya-un: To-ca ta-can-tu kin
o-ma-ni-pi, He-na wa-ste wi-ca-ki-ca-ke kta.

It was the most sorrowful, solemn occasion Jennee
had ever witnessed. Her eyes, dark and wet, never left
the coffin.

Everybody attended the funeral: the young men,
those who often had to switch back and forth between
Dakotah speech and English because of lack of vocabulary, those young men came to witness the mortal end
of the withered old man; a couple of old women, now
wrinkled and gray, came because they remembered the
times when Ed's laughter was strong and he had made
love to them when he was drunk and happy; the BIA
superintendent, a red-haired man from Georgia, the last
of eight such officials the old man had fought, attended
the last rites out of a grudging respect. And others went
out of a kind of courtesy that only the aged command:
the storekeeper; two white schoolteachers who on different occasions had invited Ed to their classrooms to
tell "legends" to the students; Willard Ree, who, as a

young man, had almost married Ed's daughter; even
Russell, Ed's brother just home from an eight-year sentence served out at the state penitentiary in Sioux Falls.
It was clearly time to behave properly, a time of significance, a time when life must be substantiated and death
lamented, a time when the disorder, the pride, and the
cruelty of human existence gives way to symbol.

IV

Because of the significance of such symbols, and, in this
case, the significance of ancestors, it must be said that
Ed had been simply born to the matter of constancy in
the lives of others. It took the form of politics. His father, Bowed Head, a man of great charm and oratorical
skill, was the first councilman elected by the people after
the 1934 Reorganization Act; thus, Ed spent a lifetime
listening to the discussions of tribal organization, the
importance of the old ways, the changes that could be
expected, the stories of past glories and the men and
women who had participated in them, the hopes for a
future of dignity in the white man's world.

He was clearly a part of those times, and he always
remembered when he rode with his father and uncles
from the Little Moreau on the Cheyenne River Sioux
reservation to the place white people came to call Bear
Butte. And the memory of their two-day approach to
that awesome prairie configuration never left him. The
butte, he would tell later, rose, dark and shadowy, from

the flatness of the land some distance from the place where the earth began to turn red, superimposing itself against the sky and sun. The riders saw it first from over the right shoulder, then the left. And, as they came upon it the second day, the grass beneath it turned dark green and marshy. It was here, he would say, that the great Dakotah councils often took place, when people from all of the bands convened as great and important issues arose. It was here that Crazy Horse, Sitting Bull, White Lance, Leader Charge, Gall, and all the others met and decided, "We will fight the white man another time." Ed saw this place become in his lifetime merely a place where tourists stopped, gazed at the scenery, and dropped half-eaten tuna sandwiches.

It must be recalled, too, that Ed's childhood was a time when the remnants of a pitiless past still existed in the minds of the people; reservation days of life in weather-beaten shacks grudgingly erected in small circles around the Agency; long lines of thin men and dull-eyed children waiting to receive their rations; people sitting quietly in churches hour after hour to escape the wind and cold. It was a time when the shadows of the fifty-foot-high board fence still encircled the Agency, reminders that this place had been a prison camp back in the days when there was a "bounty" on Indians who escaped back to the "wild" life on the plains. Ed's childhood and youth were made up of the collective generational memories of those swift, astonishing changes.

V

From this childhood, the young man grew to be a political man. It was not that Edmund was ambitious, nor that he wanted recognition; it was not even that he was expected to "make something of himself." More simply, he was born to the matter of politics and there was no escaping it. He sat in council meetings, even as a young man, and listened to the problems brought before that deliberating body, and tried to be useful. Sometimes he succeeded, sometimes he didn't.

On the day that the people of his district were asked by the Bureau of Reclamation and the United States Government to approve the construction of a huge dam on their lands to control the Missouri River for power, Ed voted against it.

"The river," he said in council, "is like the blood flowing through your arm. It cannot be stopped up . . . even for a short period of time . . . because an infection will set in. It should not be done."

But Ed was practically alone in his disapproval. And the dam was built.

He was not bitter that he had lost, because he did not think of it in personal terms. But he was sad. He reflected upon a similar time, twenty-six years before, when his people were told that they must accept U.S. citizenship for themselves, the people of the Sioux nation, the Dakotapi. At that time, also, Edmund's father gave long impassioned speeches in the tradition of the grandfathers, and he said, "It is unusual to be awarded citizenship in this manner, and it is not a practice that is widely accepted among us.

"The white man has unusual customs," he said. "He does not understand what it means to possess a birthright."

And he always ended these speeches by declaring, "To be a Dakotah, you must be born a Dakotah. Of the blood! Of the ancestors! We do not give that away, nor do we accept anything else."

But the citizenship celebrations took place anyway. And the women wrapped themselves in shawls made out of U.S. flags. And they wrapped their infants in red, white, and blue cloths, and they danced to beautiful songs. "*Oyate ki ikpaso a u welo, heyapelo,*" they sang, and "*Tunkashila yapi, tawapaha ki han oihanke śni (he) nanjin kte lo.*"

Often, Ed shook his head and smiled at the irony of the relationship established between the white man and the people of his tribe. He had come to understand the betrayal in such a relationship. It was this recognition which gave substance to his human existence.

VI

Jennee slept poorly the night of the old man's death. She awakened at every little sound and imagined that she heard creaking of doors and floor joists. She dreamed of Ed riding the prairie and returning home with the news of where the *tipsila* was in bloom. But when she went to the place he described, she could not find the small turnips. She was sure that they were there, because Ed had told her so. But she could never, never find them. She awoke with a start each time this dream recurred.

Finally, toward dawn, she got up and went out to the barn, where she untied Ed's rifle from its place on the post. She took it into the house and put it with some things which would eventually be collected for the "give-away." It was then that she wrapped the old man's pipe and got it ready to lay beside him in his white man's grave.

A Child's Story

He came slowly, upright and tall in the rich, tooled saddle, smiling just a little in that gentle, knowing way she remembered, careful, graceful, a rhythmic rider, soundless, and inexpressively perfect. He didn't look at her, but she knew that he saw her and was there, in fact, especially because she had come with the child.

She was conscious of the weight of the child as she watched the swinging fringes of his buckskin jacket, back and forth, and she wondered why he was wearing buckskin when it was so oppressively hot. She felt suddenly stifled, like the times she sat in the darkness of Saint Anne's Chapel, felt him close to her, and listened to his soft voice as he sang the white man's religious songs.

The intransigent heat blurred her vision, and she thought she saw an elk looming beside the mounted figure, yet all she could see of it was the large white eye, and then it seemed to fade away. Her body felt stiff and old.

She watched the motion of the bay horse as it drew nearer. It was a scornful animal, monstrous and solitary, awkward among the other horses, now closed in and stamping, becoming wild in its eyes like a huge bird single-mindedly blinking against the wind. The rider leaned back and then forward with the bay's lunge, and both the man and the horse formed a black, blanketing shadow which she felt upon her. A gust of hot wind, cleanly scented by the buffalo grass of the Dakota prairie ruffled her heavy dark hair, and she thought she heard the words ". . . whatever is certain . . ." as if they were carried on the wind.

It seemed to take a long time for the shadow to slowly envelop her. She felt a vague, helpless desire to weep, but she could not. Fascinated, she watched as she let him sweep the child from her arms and begin the ritualistic drama, absorbed in the sound and the motion of it, desolate because she could neither remember nor understand it. She was overcome with a terrible longing for something untraceable from the past, yet he was part of the past. Was her longing for him not over with? Why didn't he leave so that her dignity and calm and serenity could return to her? Her consciousness of the ritual was sharpened by the quick, staccato beat of the bay's hooves upon the hot, hard earth. She tried to utter responses to the ritual, but she could only feel sullen and diffuse and inarticulate as the dust rose around her ankles. Rooted into the wind and the earth, as she supposed she had once been rooted to him, she watched him ride among the other horsemen, who stilled their mounts and gave way for him, their eyes conspiring to see whatever was in the past. And she heard their celebration, "I am the elk." The stamping bay and the tall, male figure held their eyes, and the man held the infant at arm's length, riding around the barren grounds, saying the ageless words which she barely remembered, perhaps never knew.

Inexplicably, idiotically, she felt the unspeakable urge to laugh. For just a moment she was reminded of Father Giesen, that priest at the mission school who always paced between the buildings after the supper hour, reading his breviary in a strident, compelling voice, as though it were not enough to contemplate silently the powers that rested within the words.

But none of the words in either case seemed to make sense. And as she listened, she knew that she could not laugh, as she had not been able to cry.

She felt herself move just a little to the hoofbeats, as if convulsed by the sounds of some far-off drums. She could hear, faintly, the voice of Amos Flying Crow shouting, "*Wacipo . . . wacipo . . . !*" and she could almost see him walking around the powwow circle, his arms raised, beckoning the dancers to "come on and dance." And it was then that the memory of them together became intense and the intensity became pain and the pain became anguish. She remembered going slowly around in the dance with him, around the drums and the fires, in time around the drums, together, her heels and his stepping in time, together. She had felt, even then ". . . whatever is certain. . . ."

The rider kept repeating, "This is my daughter," as he held the infant at arm's length toward the crowd, and the murmurs from the faceless riders affirmed his statement. *Hechetu.*

And then he did the unexpected. He stood up in the heavy stirrups and leaned over as if to help the child reach the ground. The blanket loosened and touched the earth.

No. Wait. She wanted to cry out. But she stood, mute, until she saw the small legs dangling, unable to stand straight, the tiny, moccasined toes involuntarily snubbing back and forth in the dirt. Afraid, her throat hot, she ran forward into the deepened shadow and grasped the child around the belly.

She held the infant close and stood motionless, breathless. The face and eyes of the buckskin-clad rider came toward her, and she felt suddenly warm. She caught a sagelike odor from his straight black hair, and she felt helpless for just a moment as the elk-bone ornament tied around his neck swung toward her.

Somehow, with great effort, she stepped back, softly, so that he could not reach her. Her breath came back and her vision was once again momentarily blurred. She could see the dark shape of the man getting darker as his horse stepped sideways, away from her, into the shadow. There was just an instant more when she felt her eyes getting hot and dry, and she felt afraid. But the feeling passed quickly.

Finally, she knew the certainty of ". . . whatever is certain." The past is always the past as it is always the present.

She heard herself whisper, "Listen! Listen!" into the infant's warm blanket, her ears straining to the echoes of a stillness she had not known before.

A Good Chance

I

When I got to Crow Creek I went straight to the Agency, the place they call "the Fort," and it was just like it always has been to those of us who leave often and come home now and then: mute, pacific, impenitent, concordant. I drove slowly through the graveled streets until I came to a light blue HUD house.

"I'm looking for Magpie," I said quietly to the little boy who opened the door at Velma's place and looked at me steadily with clear brown eyes. We stood and regarded one another until I, adultlike, felt uncomfortable, and so I repeated, "Say, I'm looking for Magpie. Do you know where he is?"

No answer.

"Is your mother here?"

After a few moments of looking me over, the little boy motioned me inside.

"Wait here," he said.

He went down the cluttered hallway and came back with a young woman wearing jeans and a cream-colored ribbon shirt and carrying a naked baby covered only with rolls of fat. "I'm Amelia," she said, "do you want to sit down?"

The small, shabby room she led me into was facing east, and the light flooded through the window, making everything too bright, contributing to the uneasiness we felt with each other as we sat down.

"I need to find Magpie," I said, "I've really got some good news for him, I think," and I pointed to the brief-case I was carrying. "I have his poems and letter of acceptance from a University in California where they want him to come and participate in the fine arts program they have started for Indians."

"You know, then, that he's on parole, do you?" she asked, speaking quickly, with assurance. "I'm his wife, but we haven't been together for a while." She looked at the little boy who had opened the door, motioned for him to go outside, and after he had left, she said softly, "I don't know where my husband is, but I've heard that he's in town somewhere."

"Do you mean in Chamberlain?"

"Yes. I live here at the Agency with his sister, and she said that she saw him in town . . . quite a while ago."

I said nothing.

"Did you know that he was on parole?"

"Well, no . . . not exactly," I said hesitantly. "I haven't kept in touch with him, but I heard that he was in some kind of trouble. In fact, I didn't know about you. He didn't tell me that he was married, though I might have suspected that he was."

She smiled at me and said, "He's gone a lot. It's not safe around here for him, you know. His parole officer really watches him all the time, and so, sometimes, it is just better for him not to come here. Besides," she said, looking down, absentmindedly squeezing the rolls of fat on the baby's knees, "we haven't been together for a while."

Uncomfortably, I folded and unfolded my hands and tried to think of something appropriate to say. The baby started to cry as though, bored with all this, he needed to hear his own voice. It was not an expression of pain or hunger. He rolled his tongue against his gums and wrinkled his forehead, but when his mother whispered something to him, he quieted immediately and lay, passive, in her lap.

"But Magpie would not go to California," she said, her eyes somehow masking something significant that she thought she knew of him. "He would never leave here now, even if you saw him and talked to him about it."

"But he did before," I said, not liking the sound of my own positive, defensive words. "He went to the university in Seattle."

"Yeah, but . . . well, that was before," she said as though to finish the matter.

"Don't you want him to go?" I asked.

Quickly, she responded, "Oh, it's not up to me to say. He is gone from me now," and she moved her hand to her breast, "I'm just telling you that you are in for a disappointment. He no longer needs the things that people like you want him to need," she said positively.

When she saw that I didn't like her reference to "people like you" and the implication that I was interested in the manipulation of her estranged husband, she stopped for a moment and then put her hand on my arm. "Listen," she said, "Magpie is happy now, finally; he is in good spirits, handsome and free and strong. He sits at the drum and sings with his brothers, and he's okay now. When he was saying all those things against the government and against the council he became more and more ugly and embittered, and I used to be afraid for him. But I'm not now. Please, why don't you just leave it alone now?"

She seemed so young to know how desperate things had become for her young husband in those days and I was genuinely moved by her compassion for him and for a few moments neither of us spoke. Finally, I said, "But I have to see him. I have to ask him what he wants to do. Don't you see that I have to do that?"

She leaned back into the worn, dirty sofa and looked at me with cold hatred. Shocked at the depth of her reaction, I got up and went outside to my car. The little boy who had opened the door for me appeared at my elbow, and as I opened the car door, he asked, "If you find him, will you come back?"

"No," I said, "I don't think so."

I had the sense that the little boy picked up a handful of gravel and threw it after my retreating car as I drove slowly away. When I pulled around the corner, I glanced over my shoulder and saw that he was still standing there, watching my car leave the street: he was small, dark, closed in that attitude of terrible resignation I recognized from my own childhood, and I knew that resignation to be the only defense, the only immunity in a world where children are often the martyrs. That fleeting glimpse of my own past made me even more certain that Magpie had to say yes or no to this thing, himself . . . that none of us who knew and loved him could do it for him.

II

Home of the Hunkpati, proclaimed a hand-lettered sign hanging over the cash register at the café. It could not be said to be an inaccurate proclamation, as all of us who perceived the movement of our lives as emanating from this place knew, only an incomplete one. For as surely as the Hunkpati found this their home, so did the Isianti, the Ihanktowai, even the Winnebagoes, briefly, and others. Even in its incompleteness, though, it seemed to me to be ne plus ultra, the superstructure of historiography which allows us to account for ourselves, and I took it as an affirmation of some vague sort. In a contemplative mood, now, I sat down in a booth and ordered a cup of what turned out be the bitterest coffee I'd had since I left Santa Fe. "*Aa-a-eee-e, pe juta sapa,*" I could hear my uncle saying.

I thought about the Hunkpati and all the people who had moved to this place and some who were put in prison here as great changes occurred and as they maintained an accommodation to those changes. The magic acts of white men don't seem to work well on Indians, I thought, and the stories they tell of our collective demise have been greatly exaggerated; or, to put it into the vernacular of the myth tellers of my childhood, "*Heha yela owi hake,*" this the appropriate ending to the stories which nobody was expected to believe anyway.

I was thinking these things so intently I didn't notice the woman approaching until she was standing behind the booth, saying, "They gave me your note at the Bureau of Indian Affairs office. You wanted to see me?"

"Yes," I said from the great distance of my thoughts, having nearly forgotten my search for the young poet I wished to talk to about his great opportunity. As I looked up into her sober, intent face it all seemed unimportant, and for a moment I felt almost foolish.

Remembering my mission, I said solicitously, "Thank you for coming," and asked her to sit down across the table from me.

"Are you Salina?"

"Yes."

"This place here didn't even exist when I was a child," I told her, "the town that we called 'the Fort' in those days lay hidden along the old creek bed, and this prairie above here was the place where we gathered to dance in the summer sun."

"I know," she said, "my mother told me that we even had a hospital here then, before all this was flooded from the Oahe Dam. She was born there in that hospital along the Crow Creek."

We sat in thoughtful remembrance, scarcely breathing, with twenty years' difference in our ages, and I thought: Yes, I was born there, too, along that creek bed in that Indian hospital which no longer exists, in that Agency town which no longer exists except in the memories of people who have the capacity to take deeply to heart the conditions of the past. And later my uncle offered me to the four grandfathers in my grandmother's lodge, even though it was November and the snow had started and I was taken into the bosom of a once large and significant, now dwindling family; a girl-child who, in the old days, would have had her own name.

Abruptly, she said, "I don't know where Magpie is. I haven't seen him in four days."

"I've got his poems here with me," I said, "and he has a good chance of going to a fine arts school in California, but I have to talk with him and get him to fill out some papers. I know that he is deeply interested . . ."

"No, he isn't," she broke in. "He doesn't have those worthless, shitty dreams anymore."

"Don't say that, Salina. This is a good chance for him."

"Well, you can think what you want," and she turned her dark eyes on me, "but have you talked to him lately? Do you know him as he is now?"

"I know he is good. I know he has such talent . . ."

"He's Indian," she said as though there was some distinction I didn't know about. "And he's back here to stay this time."

She sat there all dressed up in her smart gray suit and her black, shiny fashion boots, secure in the GS-6 bureau secretarial position, and I wondered what she knew about "being Indian" that accounted for the certainty of her response. Was it possible that these two women with whom I had talked today, these two lovers of Magpie, one a wife and the other a mistress, could be right about all of this? I wondered silently. Is it possible that the drama of our personal lives is so quiescent as to be mere ceremony, whose staging is predictable, knowable? In the hands of those who love us are we mere actors mouthing their lines? Magpie, I thought, my friend, a brother to me, who am I, who are they, to decide these things for you?

Near defeat in the face of the firm resolve of these two women, almost resigned, with folded hands on the table, I looked out the window of the café and saw the lines of HUD houses, row upon row, the design of government bureaucrats painted upon the surface of this long-grassed prairie and I remembered the disapproving look of the little boy who threw gravel at my car and I found the strength to try again.

"Would you drive into Chamberlain with me?" I asked.

She said nothing.

"If he is Indian as you say, whatever that means, and if he is back here to stay this time, and if he tells me that, himself, I'll let it go. But, Salina," I urged, "I must talk to him and ask him what he wants to do. You see that, don't you?"

"Yes," she said finally, "he has a right to know about this . . . but you'll see . . ."

Her heels clicked on the brief sidewalk in front of the café as we left, and she became agitated as she talked. "After all that trouble he got into during the protest at Custer when the courthouse was burned, he was in jail for a year. He's still on parole, and he will be on parole for another five years . . . and they didn't even prove anything against him! Five years! Can you believe that? People, these days, can commit murder and not get that kind of a sentence."

She stopped to light a cigarette before she opened the car door and got in.

As we drove out of "the Fort" toward town, she said, "Jeez, look at that," and she pointed with her cigarette to a huge golden eagle tearing the flesh from some carcass which lay in the ditch alongside the road.

I thought, As many times as I've been on this road

in my lifetime, I've never seen an eagle here before. I've never seen one even near this place . . . *ma tuki* . . .

III

Elgie was standing on the corner near the F & M Bank as we drove down the main street of Chamberlain, and both Salina and I knew, without speaking, that this man, this good friend of Magpie's, would know of his whereabouts. We looked at him as we drove past, and he looked at us, neither giving any sign of recognition. But when we went to the end of the long street, made a U-turn, and came back and parked the car, Elgie came over and spoke: "I haven't seen you in a long time," he said as we shook hands.

"Where you been?" he asked as he settled himself in the back seat of the car, "New Mexico?"

"Yes."

"I seen the license plates on your car," he said, as if in explanation. There might have been more he wanted to say, but a police car moved slowly to the corner where we were parked and the patrolman looked at the three of us intently and we pretended not to notice.

I looked down at my fingernails, keeping my face turned away, and I thought, This is one of those towns that never changes. You can be away twenty minutes or twenty years and it's the same here. I remembered a letter that I had read years before, written by a former mayor of this town, revealing his attitude toward Indians. He was opposing the moving of the Agency, flooded out by the Fort Randall Power Project, to his town:

April 14, 1954

Dear U.S. Representative:

I herewith enclose a signed resolution by the city of Chamberlain and a certified copy of a resolution passed by the Board of County Commissioners of Brule County, So. Dak. The County Commissioners are not in session so I could not get a signed resolution by them. As I have advised you before, we have no intentions of making an Indian comfortable around here, especially an official. We have a few dollar diplomats that have been making a lot of noise and trying to get everyone that is possible to write you people in Washington that they wanted the Indians in here, but the fact is that 90 percent of the people are strongly opposed to it and will get much more so, if this thing comes in. Anybody who rents them any property will have to change his address and I wouldn't want the insurance on this building. We do not feel that this town should be ruined by a mess like this and we do not intend to take it laying down irregardless of what some officials in Washington may think.

H.V.M., Mayor

That same spring my uncle Narcisse, thirty-seven years old, affable, handsome, with a virtuous kind of arrogance that only Sioux uncles can claim, was found one Sunday morning in an isolated spot just outside of town with "fatal wounds" in his throat. This city's coroner and those investigating adjudged his death to be an "accident," a decision my relatives knew to be ludicrous and obscene. Indians killing and being killed did not warrant careful and ethical speculation, my relatives said bitterly.

The patrol car inched down the empty street, and I turned cautiously toward Elgie. Before I could speak, Salina said, "She's got some papers for Magpie. He has a chance to go to a writers' school in California."

Always tentative about letting you know what he was really thinking, Elgie said, "Yeah?"

But Salina wouldn't let him get away so noncommittally. "*Ozela*," she scoffed. "You know he wouldn't go!"

"Well, you know," Elgie began, "one time when Magpie and me was hiding out after that Custer thing, we ended up on the Augustana College campus. We got some friends there. And he started talking about freedom, and I never forgot that, and then, after he went to the pen, it became his main topic of conversation . . . freedom. He wants to be free, and you can't be that, man, when they're watching you all the time. Man, that freak that's his parole officer is some mean watchdog."

"You think he might go for the scholarship?" I asked hopefully.

"I don't know. Maybe."

"Where is he?" I asked.

A truck passed, and we waited until it had rumbled on down the street. In the silence that followed no one spoke.

"I think it's good that you come," Elgie said at last, "because Magpie, he needs some relief from all this," he waved his hand, "this constant surveillance, constant checking up, constant association. In fact, that's what he always talks about: 'If I have to associate with *wasichus*,' he says, 'then I'm not free . . . there's no liberty in that for Indians.' You should talk to him now," Elgie went on earnestly, eyeing me carefully. "He's changed. He's for complete separation, segregation, total isolation from the *wasichus*."

"Isn't that a bit too radical? Too unrealistic?" I asked.

"I don't know," he said, hostility rising in his voice, angry, perhaps, that I was being arbitrary and critical about an issue we both knew had no answer. "Damn if I know . . . is it?"

"Yeah," said Salina, encouraged by Elgie's response. "And just what do you think it would be like for him at that university in California?"

"But it's a chance for him to study, to write. He can find a kind of satisfying isolation in that, I think."

After a few moments, Elgie said, "Yeah, I think you're right." A long silence followed his conciliatory remark, a silence which I didn't want to break, since everything I said sounded too argumentative, authoritative.

We sat there, the three of us, and I was hoping that we were in some kind of friendly argreement. Pretty soon Elgie got out of the back seat and shut the door; he walked around to the driver's side and leaned his arms on the window.

"I'm going to walk over to the bridge," he said, "it's about three blocks down there. There's an old, white, two-story house on the left side just before you cross the bridge. Magpie's brother, he just got out of the Nebraska State Reformatory and he's staying there with his old lady and that's where Magpie is."

At last! Now I could really talk to him and let him make this decision for himself.

"There's things about this, though," Elgie said. "Magpie shouldn't be there, see, because it's a part of the condition of his parole that he stays away from friends and relatives and ex-cons and just about everybody. But jeez . . . this is his brother."

"Wait until just before sundown, and then come over," he directed. "Park your car at the service station just around the block from there and walk to the back entrance of the house and then you can talk to Magpie about all this."

"Thanks, Elgie" I said.

We shook hands, and he turned and walked down the street, stopping to light a cigarette, a casual window shopper.

IV

Later, in the quiet of the evening dusk, Salina and I listened to our own breathing and the echoes of our footsteps as we walked toward the two-story house by the bridge where Elgie said we could find Magpie. We could see the water of the Missouri River, choppy and dark, as it flowed in a southwesterly direction, and the wind rose from the water, suddenly strong and insistent.

The river's edge, I knew, was the site of what the Smithsonian Institution had called an "extensive" and "major" archaeological "find," as they had uncovered the remains of an old Indian village during the flooding process for the Oahe Dam. The "find" was only about a hundred yards from the house which was now Magpie's hiding place. The remains of such a discovery, I thought, testify to the continuing presence of ancestors, but this thought would give me little comfort as the day's invidious, lamentable events wore on.

Salina was talking, telling me about Magpie's return to Crow Creek after months in exile and how his relatives went to Velma's house and welcomed him home. "They came to hear him sing with his brothers," she told me, "and they sat in chairs around the room and laughed and sang with him."

One old uncle who had taught Magpie the songs felt that he was better than ever, that his voice had a wider range, was deeper, more resonant, yet high-pitched, sharp and keen to the senses at the proper moments. The old uncle, said Salina, had accepted the fact of Magpie's journey and his return home with the knowledge that there must always be a time in the lives of young men when they move outward and away, and in the lucky times, they return.

As she told me about the two great-uncles' plans for the honor dance, I could see that this return of Magpie's was a time of expectation and gratitude. Much later, I could see that this attitude of expectancy, a habit of all honorable men who believe that social bonds are deep and dutiful, was cruelly unrealistic. For these old uncles, and for Magpie, there should be no expectation.

Several cars were parked in the yard of the old house as we approached, and Salina, keeping her voice low, said, "Maybe they're having a party ... that's all we need."

But the silence which hung about the place filled me with apprehension, and when we walked in the back door, which hung open, we saw people standing in the kitchen, and I asked carefully, "What's wrong?"

Nobody spoke, but Elgie came over, his bloodshot eyes filled with sorrow and misery. He stood in front of us for a moment and then gestured for us to go into the living room. The room was filled with people sitting in silence, and, finally, Elgie said quietly, "They shot him. They picked him up for breaking the conditions of his parole and they put him in jail and ... they shot him."

"But, why?" I cried. "How could this have happened?"

"They said they thought he was resisting and that they were afraid of him."

"Afraid?" I asked incredulously, ". . . but . . . but . . . was he armed?"

"No," said Elgie, seated now, his arms resting on his knees, his head down. "No, he wasn't armed."

I held the poems tightly in my hands, pressing my thumbs, first one and then the other, against the smoothness of the cardboard folder.

Bennie

In 1899, Eva gave birth to her third son. It was spring, the rains had come and the prairie grass was bright and green. Like most Isianti of her generation, Eva looked hopefully toward the future for her son. She was ready to go to the Christian church with her husband, Ben, a novice politician of the tribe, who had attended Christian school and had learned to read and write the English language. She was ready to offer the child (as his brothers had been offered) to the white man's Father.

When the baby was a few days old, a brief marital argument ensued as Ben prepared an eagle feather, stroking it and wrapping its stem in red yarn, putting it carefully into the baby's blankets.

"I want to take him to Grassrope," Ben said to his wife.

"You must not make it hard for our boy," Eva admonished her husband, meaning that to live in two cultures was these days a difficult matter for Indians, and it was the time now to make the choice to reject Indian ways and become a part of the white man's way. It was either/or. That was Eva's thinking. It was, you see, that time in history when Indians were thought to be the "vanishing race." It was before Collier's 1934 Indian Reorganization Act. But, more significantly, perhaps, it was only nine years after the Wounded Knee Massacre, the killing event which was to symbolize the Final Conquest.

"You cannot raise him Indian way," said Eva. And she turned away in a pretense that the matter was settled.

In a few days, then, and alone, Ben carried the infant to the home of old Grassrope, the traditional headman of the tribe, for his blessing.

"You are lucky to have a third son," said the old pipe carrier. "I wish for you and your wife continued fertility."

Grassrope thought of his own sons, all dead in infancy. Sometimes, standing in the wagon tracks just inside the gate near the burial mounds of his children, he could sense in the air or in the vast distance toward the river and beyond, the presence of those sudden, brief, precious lives. He had adopted a boy, a child who became, then, his only significant link to future generations. He looked at the father and son before him and knew how important such a relationship could be.

"We wish to call the boy by my Christian name," said the father tentatively.

"Benjamine. Benjamine, the second, I think is the way they say it."

The old pipe carrier was silent. He had expected that the child would be named in the traditional way, that he would have an Isianti name, that he would be linked in language forever with his grandfathers. He held the eagle feather reverently and waited.

"We call him Bennie," said the father, and then he gave the time that the boy was born, a few minutes before dawn. He said that Eva had been in her bed for three days, that it was an extremely difficult birth. Grassrope carefully placed the eagle feather on the buffalo skull altar and began to pray.

Quietly, Grassrope's wife brought in the sacred food. Three bowls. One of dried deer meat pounded into meal, one bowl of corn, also ground, and the third bowl of dried chokecherry meal. Each bowlful of meal was smoothed and pressed so that the surface was flat, perfect.

"How is Eva?" the pipe carrier's wife asked innocently.

"She is fine," replied Ben. "She has plenty of milk for the baby and her face is full."

He thought guardedly of Eva, still lying in her birthing bed, unable or unwilling to get up and move about the house, as she had done when the two older boys were born. He looked down at the small form in his arms. The baby was sleeping. The naming ceremony and the baptism, then, took place almost in isolation and as though there were no familial consensus, and, thus, no communal commentary, ordinarily so much a part of such an event. Grassrope, a man of the horse and buffalo days, knew that it was his function to support and honor those who brought children into an uncertain world to face the inconsistencies of contemporary life, and he made no burdensome inquiries.

The child who received Grassrope's blessings that day remained a still, quiet, sleeping baby, and when he was a year old, he was unable to sit up by himself. Eva would hold him on her knee, watch his head bobble to one side, and say, "Bennie, why don't you sit up? Sit up, Bennie, and be a big boy."

Then she would coo in his ear and he would smile at her with soft, loving eyes and she would forgive him. Sometimes she would force him to sit up, putting pillows on each side of his body and in front of him so that he would not fall on his face, but even then his spine would not hold him upright and his limp neck would list to one side or the other and his head would hang sideways forlornly. The little Bennie never complained, seldom cried, and he would watch his mother's movements about the room with bright, loving eyes.

The muscles in Bennie's arms and hands failed to develop properly, and he could not feed himself nor play with his toys. His older brothers attended him at the table, holding him and spooning nourishment into his gaping mouth.

Bennie seemed to understand everything that was said to him, and his loving father talked to him earnestly in the evenings when he came in from his work with the horses and cattle. Bennie did not respond with language, only with his eyes and his smile. At the very beginning the family did not worry about the fact that Bennie seemed to develop more slowly than the other children had. After all, each child must be allowed to be himself. Later, however, they took him to the Public Health Hospital, where the doctors simply shook their heads.

Bennie's cheerfulness brought them all great joy, and it wasn't until Eva became pregnant again that they began to concern themselves that she would not be able to do everything for Bennie and carry him everywhere with her. They began to wish that Bennie could help himself. The older brothers sometimes became impatient with the helpless one, and in their frustration, they would say, "You have been lazy long enough, Bennie. You must learn to help yourself," and they would go off without wiping the spittle from his chin, or they would leave him alone for long periods of time.

One day when Bennie was nearly four years old, his father hooked a pair of striking bay horses to the wagon, loaded a few provisions for the day, and took the entire family on a fishing outing to the west bend in the river, where the bullheads were known to be a good catch. This was a great occasion, since it was Ben's habit and preference to fish alone, and he seldom asked his sons and Eva to join him in this activity.

Eva was sitting contentedly along the shore, with

Bennie sitting beside her leaning on her for support, when the eldest son approached.

"I feel sorry that Bennie can't fish. Can I take him over to the bank where I have my fishing pole set and teach him?" he asked.

Eva looked down at Bennie, who smiled eagerly, the skin around his mouth stretched tight, accentuating his high cheekbones and making his face take on a translucent look, somehow pale and beautiful. He started to make noises that indicated he wanted to go with his brother, and the saliva oozed from the corners of his mouth.

"Come on, little helpless one," said the brother. "Come and I will teach you how to catch a bullhead."

He grabbed Bennie and lifted him, carrying him high in his arms. When they got to the place where the brother had set his line, they found some room on the bank, made a comfortable place to sit, and Bennie watched as his brother pulled the line out of the water.

"See," the older brother said. "Look at this. What I do is I put a grasshopper or a worm on this hook. Like this. And I throw the line way out there."

He pushed what was left of the white, water-soaked worm off the hook and tediously baited it again, squishing a new fat worm into little bunches on the hook. Bennie watched, his mouth hanging open. He began to laugh as his brother took the line a few steps away, held it carefully, and gave it a great heave out into the water.

"Watch," said the brother, "watch, and you will see a fish come up there and try to get this worm that we just put on the hook, here. It's a good fresh worm, ennit?"

He sat down then and gathered Bennie into his lap. The two brothers sat quietly, their heads touching as they held on to each other, little Bennie's arms dangling in spite of himself. They looked out into the shiny glare of the water, scanning the surface where the hook and the worm had splashed and disappeared. They could hear something that sounded like a cricket in the grass behind them. "*Ah-nah-go-p-ta,*" said the older brother as his arms encircled Bennie's frail body. Together, they watched and waited, listening.